I'm a V

Bernadette Leach

Attic Press

Dublin

First Published in 1992 by
Attic Press
4 Upper Mount Street
Dublin 2

British Library Cataloguing in Publication Data
Leach, Bernadette
  I'm a Vegetarian
  I. Title II Series
  823.914 [J]

ISBN 1- 85594- 040- X

Cover Design: Luly Mason
Origination: Attic Press
Printing: The Guernsey Press Co. Ltd,

This book is published with the assistance of The Arts Council/ An Chomhairle Ealaíon.

BERNADETTE LEACH has lived in Cork since 1983 with her husband and five children. She is currently working on a second novel for teenage girls.

Acknowledgments

Without my family there wouldn't have been the
support or the ideas. Without my friends, young and
old, there wouldn't have been the interest and
encouragment. Without Henry there wouldn't have
been a word processor. And without Attic Press it
simply wouldn't have been.

Thank you all.

For Eoin

One

What she says and what she means are two totally different things. I was late home from the cinema and she was waiting in the sitting room pretending concern, a glass of wine in one hand and a long brown cigarette in the other.

'I want to understand you,' she said. I just looked, nothing more.

'Don't give me that look. I've been worried sick and all you can do is stand there sullenly. Get up to your room now,' she yelled, throwing the cigarette into the fire and clattering the glass on to the mantelpiece. 'We'll discuss this later when you're in a better frame of mind.'

I'm convinced she thinks she's living in the middle of her own personal soap opera. Nothing is simple with her any more. So, here I am, it's eleven thirty and I can't sleep. My mother is downstairs, I can hear her pacing. My seventeen-year-old brother is still out and I'm trying to fathom why today was such a disaster.

It had begun well enough, Saturday's do. I met up with my friend Posie; she's really called Penelope but a more unlikely Penelope I have yet to meet. Mum drove us into town. Posie doesn't like my mum. She's against anyone who smokes, drinks, swears and tries to *understand* her. She much prefers her own mum, who can't drive, but cooks, keeps a really clean house *and* gives her money whenever she wants for the cinema.

'Do you talk to each other at home?' I asked her once.
'What about?' Posie replied. 'She tells me what to do.
I do it and at the weekend I get away from her and the
dogs and him.' (Him is Posie's father.)

'No later than eight,' mum had said, dropping us off.
That was fine. Well it would have been fine had we not
met up with my brother Ed and his girlfriend Charlie
(real name Charlotte). She's unbelievably shy. I don't
think I've had more than ten minutes conversation
with her in the six months that Ed has known her.

Ed suggested we have a burger. I was hungry, Posie
is always happy to eat but what we didn't take into
account was the fact that by the time we got to the
cinema we were at the end of a very long queue. I tried
ringing home to let mum know we'd be a bit late; there
was no reply. Posie called me a wimp and a creep but I
tried anyway. Since dad died mum needs reassuring, a
lot of it. I tried again. I hate that sound: when you
know exactly where the phone is, where the person
should be to hear it, then, nothing.

'If she's that worried she'll check with the cinema
and realise we're holding on for the next showing.
Come on, this is boring!' And with that Posie walked
off.

We window shopped for a bit. With four pounds
fifty there's not a lot else to do. The bus fare home is
astronomical and no amount of pretending you've
forgotten to get off at your stop will persuade the bus
driver you're genuine. I hate lying anyway. I go red
and make a mess of my words. In the end we were two
hours and forty five minutes late and I still haven't said
I'm sorry.

Posie's mum, who can't drive and who *always*

answers the phone, gave us both tea and cake. It was warm in their house, warm with the TV on and the dogs sprawled in front of the fire and Mr Owen, Posie's dad, who looks very much older than the fifty he's meant to be, lying in his chair, sleeping. We talked for a bit, mainly about the food. The film wasn't worth watching so we didn't mention it.

Posie's thirteen. I noticed today when I was sitting beside her that she smells. It's an odd, musty smell. The problem is, how can I tell her without hurting her feelings? She ought to do something about it. It's not my business, but if I were in her shoes, I know I'd rather a friend mentioned it. Posie takes offence easily. I keep thinking about it. Anyway, I didn't notice the time. As I knocked on the big oak door that dad lovingly scraped the paint off and as I walked in and saw how angry she was, I knew, before I started, that the battle was won; by her. I can't talk when I'm afraid. Posie's right. I *am* a wimp.

My mother is very tall, very glamorous, with shimmering brown hair that never goes greasy. Somehow she always gets up in time to wash it. No spots. Sometimes her skin is a bit red but that's usually when she's been crying. She cries a lot lately, easily. I can't. Even as I lie here remembering how far away dad is - the graveyard is eight miles exactly from the house - I can't cry.

Help! it's after one and tomorrow is Sunday. Yuk! Who'd want to be me? I certainly know I don't.

9

Two

'Good morning, Vanessa. Did you sleep well?'

Obviously she did. Here she is all dressed up, in jeans with an ironed crease down the leg which could cut bread, make-up on and a different glass in her hand, orange juice this time. Mum never calls me Vanessa - Nessie, Lochy, Lochness but never Vanessa, not unless she's in a really bitchy mood.

'Toast?' Mum asks, bright and breezy. I nod. Does toast need an answer? 'Yeah. Thanks.'

She frowns, she hates yeah. What does she really expect after about four hours sleep and some fundamentalist rock group that have kept me company for most of the night.

Ed walks in in his boxer shorts. He's always scratching. She frowns again.

'Ed, can you not get dressed in the morning?'

I look at him looking at her and wonder why she didn't bury dad closer to home. Brains are strange the way they suddenly come up with the most unlikely thought at the oddest time. The reason I think it just now is because Ed is so like him. Both about the same height, five foot nine or ten. Already Ed is very strong. Not that I ever saw dad in boxer shorts wandering around the kitchen. It's just that there is something familiar when Ed 'truffles' - mum's word for his poking in and out of cupboards and drawers looking for things. It reminds me of how things used to be.

'Ok. This is a project weekend,' dad would say, clapping his hands together and looking at us across the breakfast table. They were all project weekends. We bought this old house five years ago and every bit of it needed repairing, from floors to ceilings and windows, to his favourite: the front door, now newly varnished and my entrance point into so many rows recently.

Dressed in jeans and a T-shirt with the brown hair shining, she sits down as if a big announcement is going to be made. Ed, still scratching, with his hair sticking up in tufts at the top of his head, eventually stops trying to find the scissors to open the carton of orange juice and tears the top off with his teeth. I look across at mum; that frown again.

And then the explosion as Ed opens it too quickly and what looks like a gallon slops on to the tiled floor.

'For God's sake, Edward, can't you do anything without causing chaos?'

He doesn't say a word. He puts the juice down and picks up a towel which is on top of the tumble-drier in an old shopping basket.

'Don't,' she yells. 'Don't you dare. While you were lying in bed I was down here doing the washing. I've just dried that. Get some kitchen roll.'

I feel like saying that 'doing' the washing was only shoving it in the machine, waiting for half an hour and then poking it into another machine. Ed's big feet pad to the kitchen roll. He tears off some sheets and dumps them down into the mess, causing the orange juice to splash up on to the floor cupboard doors. Mum is watching. Then, getting up slowly, she leaves the room, big tears running down her make-up on to the T-shirt. Ed swears. I wonder why everything suddenly

11

has to be caught up in grand entrances and exits.

Once the kitchen is cleanish and the towel put back into the washing machine, I go upstairs and knock on her bedroom door. No answer. I knock again. There's a noise. Sobbing? Laughing? It sounds weird, so I walk in. There she is with the TV on and a video of last summer's holiday on the screen. I'd forgotten it existed. It's not possible. There he is, dad, leaping around with my uncle's little son, Ben. They're charging backwards and forwards, chasing each other like pups, playing rough and tumble for fun.

'Hi, Nessie ... I'm sorry,' she begins, looking at me.

'You're sorry ...' And then it's my turn to burst into tears. Telling her is easy when she's properly sad. She's vulnerable then, not hard. She's become really hard lately. Never before did she frown and criticise all the time. It's like living with someone brand new. They look the same but they aren't. We dry our eyes. Mum turns off the television but the video keeps on whirring - I'll do that later.

'Nessie, I need to talk to you and Ed.'

That's all right by me. I don't ask what about.

'I'll be down in a second. Would you make me a strong cup of coffee and put a teaspoon of sugar in it?' She only ever takes sugar under stress. At forty-two you can't be too careful, I suppose, not that she looks it or acts it, most of the time.

Coffee with sugar and an announcement. Maybe Sunday isn't going to be boring after all.

Three

Ed is dressed. He's not wearing the muscle top that mum loathes. In black jeans and basketball boots with the tongue flopping out he doesn't remind me of anyone. He's just my brother again. His hair is gelled back (not too much) and there's a grin on his face. He's ready to cope with whatever mood mum might be in. Will she realise that he's making a big effort?

I hand her the cup of coffee and we sit.

'My apologies, Ed. Orange juice on a floor wiped up with a towel isn't the end of the world,' she begins. Her brown eyes are still full of tears but the one thing I love about my mother even after a bout of hating her, is that she can say sorry. Ed grunts in reply. The apology is accepted even though I'm convinced that he was a bit in the wrong. Sipping at the coffee and smoking with a shaky hand, she suddenly says, 'I'm really sorry, kids. I know that this is going to come as a shock, but ...'

In the space of seconds I know that (a) she's going to die, (b) she's getting married again, (c) she's pregnant.

' ... We are going to have to move from this house.'

The relief, the pure relief. There are lots of smaller houses locally. We were warned that it was going to be a struggle buying this house and that was when dad was alive. I can remember being scared when we moved from Aylesbury to Colchester. So a smaller house will be fine, no problem.

But in the middle of my giving the kitchen a bit of a

farewell glance, with the promise of popping back now and again to check on the new owners, I hear something which doesn't quite fit in ...

'You'll love Cork.'

Cork, what's cork? It's a bottle stopper. It's a bathroom mat. I look wildly across at Ed who's shaking his head.

'You can't, mum There's me and Charlie, there's A-levels, there's University. You can't.' He looks as if he's going to hit her. I know he won't. I also know that he won't go.

'It's all right, Ed. You can stay on for the last year. I've already discussed it with Tony.' Tony, dad's brother, father of Ben, the little boy playing in the sand on the video. A very useful uncle. He's also the headmaster of Ed's school!

'Then, if you want to join us you can. Nessie and I will have everything sorted out by then.'

Hold on. Tony knows, mum knows. Ed will be slotted in so that he's not too bothered. What about me?

She looks across at me, all excited and expectant. Suddenly the prospect of a new brother or sister looks like a much more happy event.

'Ness, you'll love Ireland.'

Ireland! I want to shriek at her that leprechauns and Guinness didn't turn me pink with pleasure when I woke up this morning, nor are they about to do so at this very instant. I want to spit at her, scratch her. But all I can come out with is, 'Why?'

'Do you remember when I went away a few months ago? I said it was for a little break but I didn't mention that it was really for an interview. I didn't want to get your hopes up. Anyway, I got the job. It puts me back

14

in the mainstream. I'll be lecturing in literature.'

What is the mad woman talking about? Mainstream. What's mainstream? And lecturing? Since when did she lecture except to Ed and me when we've done something wrong. Ireland, bloody stupid Cork. No one lives in Ireland. You might go there for a holiday and come back hating the place. But at least you come back.

'What about the bombs?' I ask, in as steady a voice as I can find. It has to be some gross joke, or maybe she's gone over the edge. I cannot believe she means it.

'Oh, Nessie!' She attempts to stroke my hair. I pull back. 'That's in the North,' she rambles on. 'We're going to the South. We'll be near the sea. We can travel. Once we've sold the house and I start the job we'll be able to live more comfortably. Daddy left us well provided for but I want this as much for me as for you two. I need to start again.'

And that's it. She wants something for her. Forget me. Forget Ed. Forget Posie and my friends. Forget everything. We're going to live in some unknown country where nobody worth knowing lives.

'I'm staying with Ed.' I can feel my voice changing. I've cried once today. I'm not going to give her the satisfaction of doing it again.

She gets up. Kettle on, scrape of the spoon in the jar. I look wildly at Ed. He's shaking his head as if warning me. Dad used to do that. And then I shout it at her. 'You can't take me away. I won't ever see Dad again.'

Turning round, she looks at me as if I'm the one who's done something wrong.

'That's right, Vanessa. He's gone. You and I and Ed, we're here, we're alive, we're going to make a fresh start. I would prefer your approval but I'm afraid that whether I have it or not, we are going to Ireland.'

15

Four

July, a whole year since I became a half-orphan. Then I was twelve, now I'm thirteen. Thirteen, with a big spotty face and I feel fat all the time. Fat I could just about live with but I can't remember when I didn't wake up feeling sick. Posie says it's because I'm worried. What would she know? She's got her mum who cooks and her dad who sleeps and she's already got a replacement for me. Dorinda. Nobody can seriously be called Dorinda but she is. What makes it worse is that Dorinda is nice. She's already cured Posie's smell. She bought her some all-over spray for her fourteenth birthday and some beauty without pain skin cleanser and suddenly Posie and Dorinda no longer ask me to go to the cinema on Saturday.

Tomorrow we're getting on the plane at Heathrow and flying to Cork. I'm surprised that a plane actually lands there - I looked up Cork in the encyclopaedia. I knew I was right. All I could find was brewing and agriculture. There were other bits but they were equally boring. I've given up talking to mum. She thinks it's all some big adventure. Anyone would think we were off to New Guinea. As far as I'm concerned we might as well be. What's the difference?

I said goodbye to Ed exactly twenty minutes ago. It's eight fifteen and far too bright outside to sleep. Ed's not coming to the airport tomorrow.

'Listen Ness, you'll cry, mum will get upset and you'll start shouting again. I'll see you in October, for half-term. I promise.' I know he means it. I know he'll be there in October but what am I going to do in between?

Uncle Tony took me to the graveyard this afternoon. He put his arm around me and told me how tall I'm getting. Great ... spots, feeling sick, and now I'm going to be a giantess. Isn't life wonderful!

It's too big, the graveyard. It's hundreds and thousands of dead people. Dad should have had somewhere more exclusive. Uncle Tony started to look really sad so I tried chatting about the house. I told him how odd it is without the furniture, how funny it feels now, empty and full of echoes. I didn't tell him that I'd chipped off a tiny piece of the oak front door, which I've put into my jewellery box. Dad gave me the box for my confirmation. My gold chain is in it. The new owners won't notice a tiny piece of wood gone from their front door. It has nothing to do with them anyway. I also didn't let Tony see me pick up a smooth white pebble, which I have in my hand right now. It was lying on top of the mound, dad's grave, which is all covered up with flowers and underneath which is the only person in the world who really knew me or bothered to care about me.

In the car Uncle Tony acted all excited and enthusiastic about the move.

'We'll all be over in October, your aunt and me, Ben and Wendy.' Wendy's the baby. She cries a lot.

'Don't be too hard on your mother, Vanessa. She wants you to be happy,' he said.

The only reply that I could find in my true heart was, 'Bullshit!'

It was a very silent journey home.

17

Five

I've never been on a plane before. We're near the front and I can look down on to the sea underneath us. Little plastic trays of food and drink have been served but I'm going to be a vegetarian from today so I just took the orange juice and trifle. Mother frowned. She's on to her second gin and tonic and she looks glamorous. Her hair has been cut short. It sits round her face like a helmet and I can just see the hoop earrings glinting through. She's wearing heavy eye make-up. It looks good and she knows it.

I'm going to grow my hair until I can sit on it. I don't ever want to look like her. I know she wants me to talk to her. Tough! I've got my book and somewhere in my bag is some chocolate. I can't get my hand away in time. She puts her left hand over mine.

'Look, Nessie, we're just coming over the Irish coast. Isn't it beautiful?'

But I can't see or hear what else she's saying because where her wedding and engagement ring used to be, there's a space; there's just a slight dent left behind. I am not going to look at the Irish coast. All around there's babbling. The green uniformed hostesses have skin that either looks like ivory or is all peppered with freckles. The smell of perfume and cigarette smoke is too much.

'You can't go to the toilet now,' mum says sharply. 'The lights have gone up, look, it says *Fasten Your Seat Belt*.'

'I'm going to throw up.'

She gives one of her despairing I-really-don't-know-what-I'm-going-to-do-with-this-dreadful-child looks to the hostess. The hostess gets up, smiling.

'Come on. You've got plenty of time. That's just a safety precaution.'

I'm as tall as she is and I feel as wide as the aisle we're walking down. My head is light and I know I'm going to fill the whole aeroplane with orange juice and trifle and the two Mars bars and one bar of chocolate I've eaten in the space of an hour.

Pushing open the door of the tiny cubicle, she stands to one side to let me in. There's no time to smile, no time to say thank you. As I keep retching and throwing up what feels like a lifetime's instead of a journey's food, I wonder if it's all floating down on to some poor unsuspecting Irish person. Serve them right! There's a knock on the door. Hastily I flush the loo, stupid thing. Why can't they build bathrooms on planes?

It's the air hostess with some little sachets. I take them, smile at her and finally lock the door. The first one is a wet tissue all wrapped up in foil. Wiping my face, I begin to feel better. The next is a little pouch with a brush and toothpaste. I brush my teeth and feel closer to the strange air hostess than I've ever been to my mother. The third makes my eyes stand out. It's a sanitary towel. I know that I don't need it yet but unlike my mother the air hostess has given me the choice. Tucking it into my jeans pocket I check to make sure I've left the place tidy.

Sitting out there somewhere is my mother who pretends to understand. Without her knowing it I've met someone who really knows what the word means.

Six

Amazing! The plane didn't crash and here I am in a taxi with my mother chattering like a magpie beside me. I cannot get enthusiastic about houses and trees which look exactly the same as all other houses and trees except these ones are here and the ones I wouldn't mind seeing are hundreds of miles away.

The good thing is that I know one person in this dump. Sorcha O'Hare. She's the air hostess who treated me like a human being, not a bit of excess baggage. Imagine being called Sorcha. It beats Vanessa, Penelope, Dorinda, or any other name I've heard before. Even better, she has a sister who's my age. Her name is Aideen. They live in a place called Bishopstown. Oh God, don't let it be all churches and religion. I am really frightened and all mum can do is talk on and on, interrupting my thinking.

I'm getting very good at raising one eyebrow. Without saying a word I can get my point across. If my mother attempts to put her arm around me one more time I am going to jump out of this taxi.

'Here we are, darling. Welcome to your new abode. What do you think?' she gushes.

She is standing excitedly in front of me, sunglasses perched on top of her head, the hoopy earrings shining and bouncing around. At any minute some small-time television producer is going to yell 'Cut!' She's still in soap land, where loving daughters shout hip hip hooray, thank you for bringing me here. What do I think of it? What do I think of our new house? I think it's appalling. There's an arched front door and hundreds of tiny windows in sets of four on either side. Not only is it ridiculously big, it's yellow. Yellow stone. I cannot think of anything to say. Even my eyebrow fails to go up. I've just made it twitch instead. There's ivy creeping along everywhere and the garden is walled all around me. It's like a prison. I knew that she had flipped when she said she was moving here. This edifice proves it. Huge purple and pink bushes are clumped across the grass. It simply has to be a joke.

'How can we afford this?' It seems like a logical question but anyone would think I'd just suggested to my mother that she takes her clothes off and runs naked around the garden.

The taxi driver is trying to find change. The money looks all wrong, the notes too big, the coins quite different. Mum still hasn't answered me. Judging by the look on her face, I suspect that when she does it will be without the silly school-girl grin she adopted as soon as she saw what she calls an abode, commode more like!

On the steps up to the house are our three suitcases, mum's new leather holdall and my sports bag. The house reminds me of the TV serial *Brideshead Revisited*. We all used to love sitting down on a Sunday afternoon drinking cups of tea, eating biscuits and watching each episode. I will read the book, dad. You said I was too young then. I'm getting older. That was a long time ago.

Crunch, the taxi's gone.
'Well,' I ask again, 'how can we afford this?' I hope

my disapproval has been noticed.

At first she doesn't say anything and then, doing a pivot like a ballerina, she turns to face me.

'Vanessa.' Her face is hard as she says my name, her eyes like brown stone. 'I know you're unhappy but unhappiness is not an excuse for ill-manners or bloody-mindedness. For the whole journey from the airport that man (the taxi driver) was trying to make you feel at home. You, not me. You didn't speak to him once (I didn't hear him). You are not going to grow up a middle-class brat with ideas above your station.' (Station. Middle class. She's definitely mad.)

Cutting her off, I concentrate on the garden. I can vaguely hear her droning on but there's something else, a faint cry, a painful cry.

'Come here, Vanessa. Vanessa, I'm talking to you.'

The cry is coming from a corner, just near the front gate.

Suddenly I'm not in Ireland, Cork to be more exact. I'm not anywhere. I am deep in the bushes. They prickle and hurt. They are dry and hard. And reaching into them I touch ... a cat. I take him in my arms, he's huge and angry and my hand is covered in scratches. The whole side of his head is a mass of cuts and blood and missing bits. His coat is like the old fur my grandmother used to wear, patchy, worn.

'For heaven's sake, Vanessa, put that thing down.'

Standing up, I realise I can now look my beautiful, angry, hard mother straight in the eye.

'No, he's mine and he's hurt. What's more, I'm going to find a vet for him.'

22

Seven

Have you ever walked down a really busy street, carrying a wild animal, not knowing whether you are going the right way? If you have, we must show each other our scars sometime.

'C'mon, Puss, it'll be all right,' I try reassuring the poor creature. He smells like a bag of dirty washing. Buses roar past, leaving behind a trail of hot, smokey dust. I feel as if I'm walking through a noisy, foggy tunnel. On my right there's an enormous red building with *Bureau de change* on a placard pinned to the wall.

'Excuse me.' I say to an old lady waiting at a bus stop. 'Is there a vet nearby?'

She smiles and opens her mouth and I can't understand a word she's saying.

'Pardon?' She says it all again. It's useless. I don't understand a thing. I thank her and continue walking on.

Puss is now attempting to reduce my index finger to chopped mince. He would be black coated if he weren't so mangey. A tug on my arm. Looking at me as if I were the foreigner, the old lady guides me back the way I had come. After about two hundred yards she points to a gateway. *Veterinary Surgeon, Peter Fairhead MVB, MRCVS.* I say goodbye and thank you and turn to watch my helper pottering off up the road back to her bus stop. A bus rushes past me and I really hope that it wasn't the one my kind old lady needed.

I knock on the door marked surgery and wait. Everyone seems to have these pink and white bushes. Peter Fairhead's are almost growing into the doorway. The cat isn't struggling any more. He's limp. For the first time in weeks I don't feel sick. I feel angry. Knocking on a door with a wild animal in your arms is not easy, even when the wild animal appears to be in a coma. So the only solution is a good kick. Up until now I've been really careful of my boots. Mum insisted they were too heavy for summer. I didn't care. Posie and Dorinda had a pair and they looked great. But that was in April. It's now July. Suddenly I don't care if they end up with no toes. I give the door a mighty whack just as someone opens it.

'My cat's hurt.' He, the vet I suppose, doesn't say anything. Thank Heavens. I probably wouldn't be able to understand him either. We're now in the surgery proper. No one else seems to be around. A yelp from a kennel somewhere in the back of the house revives Puss sufficiently for him to tear at another chunk of my wrist.

'Put him there,' the vet commands.

I can understand him! I don't believe it! I put the cat on the examination table. I've never been in a vet's surgery. In all my life I have never before owned a pet. Mum isn't the greatest animal lover and dad, who used to have dogs when he was young, said it wasn't fair to keep an animal unless you really wanted one and knew how to make it welcome. I really wanted Puss.

The room smells like an operating theatre. That is one smell I will never forget. I was six and had to have my tonsils out. For months afterwards if I even got a whiff of disinfectant I used to panic. Someone ought to warn little kids about hospitals. In fact, someone ought to make sure that their little kids are allowed to walk around one, just to see how different they are from home.

'You should be ashamed of yourself. This animal has mange.'

I look. I try to appear in control. I can't say anything. 'What about these injuries? Either keep a pet or have it destroyed when it's in this condition. This is crass negligence.'

Crass negligence. Is that a disease?

'Look at his tail!'

Puss isn't quite purring but this man who is attacking me with words is gently touching and prodding the lumpy black fur as if Puss is a prize exhibit.

'Is that why you have brought him to me, to have him put down?'

All at once I find my voice. 'No ...' I sound wobbly and small. Remembering that I'm almost as tall as my mum, I begin.

'My name is Vanessa Carter. I arrived this afternoon. I don't live here. Well, I do now but I don't want to. I found Puss as soon as we arrived. I've been walking for ages.' Then, as always, the wobble turns into a sob. I hate this. 'My hands hurt, my wrists hurt and I don't even know where I live.'

If Posie had seen this performance she'd have given me an Oscar. Super Wimp, the twentieth century's answer to weak, wet and wishy washy.

Peter Fairhead has kept Puss in the surgery for a few days. He walked me back the way I'd come. We found the yellow house all right. It's probably known

25

throughout the town for being the horrible monstrosity it is.

Oh, but mother is angry with me. All the lovey dovey stuff has definitely been packed away with the cardboard boxes and chaos of the move. She couldn't send me to my room because I haven't decided where it is. So, I'm sitting here, in the garden, listening to the birds and the traffic.

I miss Ed.

Eight

'I'm a vegetarian, mother. That means I do not eat meat.'

A more stupid person it would be difficult to find, but I'm landed with her and here we are, sitting in an Indian restaurant, having walked past the vet's, over the road and into what I suppose is the town. It's not big enough to be a city but she insists that it is.

'Vanessa.' The voice again. 'The majority of Indians are vegetarians. Read the menu and choose something.'

I look. I am absolutely starving but then so are the majority of Indians probably. She's trying. Initially she wanted to go to a steak house but I got my eyebrow in working order and then she suggested here.

'Coke,' I answer.

'I beg your pardon?' When she begs my pardon she is preparing herself for something even more dangerous.

'Please,' I add.

A very long-haired Indian appears. In all my life I have never seen such a trendy looking waiter. Fascinating.

'Can I help?'

Miracle of miracles, I can understand him too. Maybe it was just the old lady who was from another planet. I notice the waiter looking oddly at the elastoplasts on my fingers and the gauzy bandages on my wrists. Mum wanted me to have a tetanus injection.

27

I want to die so I couldn't see the point.

'I'm a vegetarian,' I announce. The beautiful long-haired waiter smiles a look of such happy acceptance that I am forced to grin back.

'Then for you I have a choice of the finest vegetables and cheeses, curds and breads. You will enjoy every mouthful.'

I must confess I didn't expect such whole-hearted enthusiasm but here goes. Even mother is smiling. The food is not too spicy and I don't miss meat at all. Chewing on an onion something or other reminds me of hamburgers. Those were the good times.

'Can I ring Posie when I get back ?'

'Yes, you may.' Always the little grammatical dig. But nothing more, no heavy-duty lecture about telephone bills, important phone calls missed because I spend so long talking to my friends. Well, that's all at an end now. I don't have any friends here. Mum is eating something beefy. It smells delicious.

'What are we going to do tomorrow?' Not that I'm interested but mother is rarely silent for this long.

'Go to church, walk through Cork and think about Monday when I have to see the headmaster and you can have a quick look around the school.'

School! My stomach lurches. School! I knew it was coming, that it had to be hiding in the shadows like some night raider, but it's not until you hear the word that it really makes an impression.

'What did you say it was called again?' I don't care but the big glass of wine and the beautiful smelling food and the cool restaurant seem to have put her in better humour.

'City Community School,' she replies.

28

There she goes again insisting that this place is a city.

'Is it near?' The planet Mars would be too near at this precise moment.

'Yes, you'll be able to walk there. Oh, Nessie, you are going to love it here.'

Looking straight at her now I can see that she means it. How can she? How can she love someone else's country, their dumb University and even dumber yellow stone house? There has to be a gap in her heart. She must be sick. There's something wrong with a woman who can leave her son and husband behind.

'Everything you want is within walking distance, the Cinema, bowling, shops. That's why I was so keen on this job. Living here is going to be so much easier, not only for me but for you as well, Nessie.'

Holding up one of my damaged hands, I ask, 'How can we afford that house?'

'Nessie.'

Wait for it! After weeks of non-communication she's going to try understanding me again.

'Can I keep the cat?' I'd much rather a good old-fashioned row right now and the cat strikes me as being as good a subject as any to wrangle over.

'Yes.'

I am not going to say a word.

'Nessie! Houses here are a lot less expensive than at home.' She said it, she said the word, home. She knows she's dumped me on foreign soil.

'I've been able to put some money to one side, plus I now have the job. I promise you, everything is going to be fine.'

Her short hair really suits her.

Nine

I didn't get tetanus but I did get 'flu. How romantic, bones that ached, a hacking cough and temperatures that soared into three figures and gave me the oddest dreams. No sooner was I better than mum decided she just had to see Dublin. Sticking us both on the train, she oohed and aahed her way through the countryside. What is it about adults? I think one tree looks very much like the next, certainly one dump with used tyres is no more special than any I saw in England. She was in ecstasy.

On the positive side, Dublin is a city. At least you feel you could get lost there; I tried to, unsuccessfully of course. Mother came chasing after me and told me how clever I was to discover a side street off the beaten track. Then she proceeded to take me in and out of junk shops and spent a small fortune on a chipped jug and bowl which she's put in her bedroom.

If you could see the school that she's abandoned me in you would not believe it. This is not a school and what I'm wearing is not a uniform. The building grows like a mushroom on the road. Walking through an ordinary front door into the entrance hall is like stepping into Doctor Who's Tardis. The outside has nothing to do with the inside. It backs away for miles. There are corridors and rooms and voices and noises. What I'm wearing is too disgusting for words. It's a suit, a grey suit with a maroon shirt and black short socks. Yes, they are black and they are very short. I told mum I wouldn't wear them, so she took all my others out of the drawer. No choice! And the shoes! I've no idea where my boots are. Probably in the middle of my 'flu, when I was too delirious to notice, she hi-jacked them. So here I am in black lace-up shoes. I look like a stunted air hostess. Talking of air hostesses, I still haven't met Aideen. Her family have a cottage or something in West Cork. Apparently Sorcha's bringing her over at the weekend. I'll believe it when I see it!

It's Monday. I can't bear it. Monday, September the third. Puss/Prince went to the loo in my bedroom. Can you imagine it! After all I have done for him. The only thanks I get are fleas on my pillow and a load of pee against my dressing table. I had to clear up the mess before I set off for school. The cat's still a bit moth-eaten but Peter Fairhead (remember, the vet? It's a stupid surname seeing as he has grey hair!) told mum the cat would live to be twenty. He reckons he's around five or six and has spent his life on the road, fighting and losing. Peter's neutered the poor thing. I think I should have been consulted. Puss definitely knows he should have been asked. I just hope he remembers that he had a good sex life, once.

'Vanessa, welcome.' It's the deputy head. All my books are in my satchel. That's another weird thing: you have to buy all your books. The writing ones are called copies. We used to call them exercise books. The textbooks, the whole lot are sitting on my back, weighing me down. If they don't find me a locker soon I will go down in history as being deformed on the first day through the weight of learning.

I'm meant to be doing Italian while the others do Irish. Irish! Why does anyone have to learn Irish? It seems like an awful lot of brain space is being taken up with something not terribly useful.

'Fáilte chuig rang Breandán, Vanessa.' She said it! She is talking in a foreign language and they are looking at me. The room is very hot and very stuffy. There must be a hundred pairs of eyes watching me, waiting.

'Breandán, meet Vanessa Carter. Vanessa, this is class Breandán.' Not 2B or A or even X. Breandán! I look down.

'This is your form room, Vanessa. You will come here each morning and attend registration. Clara, you are doing the same options as Vanessa. Would you take care of her today?'

Options! That's a joke. Options imply choice. I had no choice. I couldn't do art because it clashed with science, so now I'm doing woodwork! Maybe they'll teach me how to build a gallows.

Clara scrapes back her chair from the ancient desk. She's enormous. Great. The deputy head has handed me the ugly girl so that we'll be friends and I'll take Clara off her hands. Well she can forget it. I don't even look at Clara.

'It's only the register, then I'll take you along to the maths room.' She has the sweetest voice. It lilts and rolls. I still don't look at her.

'You'll like it here. I'll take you to the Burger Bun at lunchtime. We're allowed out for an hour.'

Fixing her and her sweet voice with a stare, I say as cuttingly as possible, 'I'm a vegetarian. I couldn't possibly eat a hamburger.'

Ten

They don't pronounce their words right. I know English is being spoken but it doesn't sound right. And the history! I've been here for two hours and already I can feel them ganging up on me. Where did all the history come from? My history book is full of nightmare pictures of death and destruction. They're more like Ethiopia than Éire. Ok we're talking a hundred years ago but they are horrific. It's pure fantasy. Whenever the word Britain or British is mentioned, I feel like disappearing into my desk. We were doing the Industrial Revolution and expansionism at my old school. That was exciting. This stuff is depressing.

Clara offers me a sweet. 'No thank you. Animal fats.' I hope I sound condescending. And now it's lunchtime.
'Do you want to come for a coke? ' she asks.
'No, thanks. I'll go home for lunch.'
A gang of about eight boys and girls rush up to Clara. They drag her off, laughing and talking. Nobody said hello to me. One of the girls looks nice. She didn't even notice me.

I'm not really going home for lunch. Taking my sandwiches out into the back of the school where there are fields and tennis courts, I ignore everyone. There's a small dark-haired girl sitting on a bench. She looks harmless enough and she's not wearing the uniform. A rebel? I ask myself. I open the container and take out my cheese sandwich. It's dry and the bread is stale. Even the bread's different here. What's more, it's called a pan. It's a loaf, I want to tell the lady in the corner shop. Corner shops are very useful though. They're everywhere and they all have the most delicious ice-cream. Not that I've mentioned that to my mother. She knows how much I hate being here.

The small girl looks up. Help ! She's crying.
'You ok?' I ask.
'No.'
'Oh,' I reply. 'Your sandwiches are probably as stale as mine,' I offer jokingly. 'Do you want one?'
She looks into the box and shakes her head. I can't blame her.
'Your first day too?' I ask.
'No. I've been here before. Well, not here, but in Cork.'
She sounds all right and, more importantly, I can understand her. Some of them speak so quickly it's impossible to separate one word from the other.

On closer inspection I notice just how awful she looks. Her jersey is thin, her skirt really old fashioned.
'Does your dad work abroad or something?' It seems a reasonable question. Maybe he's a hostage in some country or other. Perhaps she's fled here for protection.
'Something like that.'
'What's your name?' I ask, trying to chew my way through my disgusting sandwich.
'Thérèse McDermot. And yours?'
I tell her. Looking around I can see a bunch of girls staring at us. I recognise one or two of them from my

class. I stare back. 'Which class are you in?' She's hard going, but she looks as pathetic as I feel.

'Cathal.'

'Why all this naming of classes? I don't understand it.'

Now she's smiling. 'I think it's meant to make us feel better. Áine is for A. Breandán, B, Cathal, C, Deirdre, D, Enda, E. Either way you're A or E but a pretty name is added to make you feel less stupid.'

I like her. 'What does your dad do?'

I don't know why I always have to know what fathers do. Mine was an accountant. Posie's works for the electricity board. Dorinda's is a librarian. Anyway, Thérèse suddenly looked suspicious. 'Mine's dead. So there's no way I can say my dad's better than yours.'

She laughs, then says solemnly, 'I'm sorry, Vanessa.'

So am I. But there's not very much I can do about it.

'I don't know what he does,' she says eventually, 'I've never met him. I'm a traveller. My mother married outside the community. After a while he left.'

Travelling sounds like fun. I know being called a gypsy carries a fairly heavy penalty from the rest of society, but if Thérèse weren't so pinched looking and her clothes so tatty, she'd be pretty.

When I get back to my desk after lunch there's no one in the classroom, but in my place is a note. 'Tinker loving Brit,' it reads.

Day one and I've already earned the undying devotion of someone. I put the note in my bag and wait. The minutes keep dragging by and then the classroom begins to fill.

'Hi!' It's Clara, still beaming, still undaunted, still fat.

'Sweet,' she offers again.

I take one. She smiles.

Eleven

Clara decided to walk back with me. We live fairly near one another.

'Clara?' I begin. She nods as she plods along. 'I got a note this afternoon.'

'A note. Who from. One of the teachers?'

'No. Hold on.' Fishing in my satchel, sack, as they call them here, I pull it out and show it to her. In her sweet voice she lets out a stream of language even Ed would only reserve for a major catastrophe. I must ask her later on why everyone swears so much here.

'Ignore it, Vanessa.'

I explain that I'd sat with Thérèse at lunch time, even though it means admitting that I didn't go home.

'Let me put you in the picture, Vanessa,' she begins, 'Wherever in this world you go, you'll find bigots. We've as fine a selection here as you have back home. Whether it's Tinker or Brit, Paddy or Fatty, they'll be there waiting in the wings.'

Looking at me hard, as if she knows I'd already labelled her 'fat', she continues. 'I haven't met Thérèse yet, but how about tomorrow? Even though you don't eat meat, you come along with her and the rest of us. At least then you'll see that some of us are all right.'

I agree, but I'm not sure Thérèse will have enough money so I must remember to bring extra.

My bedroom is tiny. I wanted this little room because it looks out on to the front of the house and I can see Prince/Puss's corner from here. He certainly seems to have adapted to domestic life very nicely, thank you. The trouble is he's decided the whole world is his toilet, starting with my room as his particularly favourite spot. Outside, the garden, he seems to feel must be kept clean and bright for play. I'd better stop calling him Prince. Puss is far more appropriate for the slob he's turning out to be. But I do love him, despite his faults.

Mrs Dineen baked brown bread while I was at school. She's the housekeeper. At least that's what mum says she likes to be called. She lives in a little house near the Cinema and cycles up to our place to clean and cook. She used to work for the family that lived here before and mum said it would be rotten not to keep her on. I think it's wrong to have servants, not that Mrs Dineen is a servant, but it feels odd having someone else in the house doing the stuff that mum used to do before. I like Mrs Dineen. She likes the cat which is more important and is trying to train him. I have a sneaking suspicion he's beyond help. But I daren't let mum into that secret.

Ed has rung twice. He and Charlie have split up and he hates it at Tony's. The baby keeps crying and Ben keeps sneaking into Ed's room and rummaging through his things. I'll warn him about the school before he comes charging over here, imagining that he can pick up the pieces and get on as normal. Learning the names of Irish mountains and rivers is no joke. I don't even know where the wretched places are. Normal feels like a very, very long time ago.

Twelve

Thérèse isn't in school today but going with Clara and her gang to the Burger Bun was a good idea. One of the boys, Damien, is very popular. Everyone except Clara is all over him. I don't want a boyfriend, but I would love to get to know Damien. He, naturally enough, ignores me. It must be my spots. All those ice-creams are erupting like cornets on my chin. I decided to try a face pack last night. It was in one of mum's old magazines, the sort that she doesn't buy now, not intellectual enough, I suppose. The recipe for this face pack sounded good enough to eat, a bit of bran, milk and a smidgeon of yogurt. I had just about mixed it together and applied the first dollop, when The Cat moved in on the mixture. I thought cats were meant to be stealthy and delicate. This one seems to have a bull elephant as a distant relative. With both front paws in the dish and his chin covered in goo, he leapt off the dressing table, taking the bowl down with him on to the new carpet. Naturally enough by the time I got round to cleaning it up, my lovely face pack had hardened. I only hope it improves the look of Puss's coat. My face and the carpet have definitely come out badly from the experiment.

And my hair isn't ready to be sat on. It is ready to be cut. I promised myself I'd grow it. I keep tying it back but it flies out of the elastic band, not in romantic little wisps, but in greasy chunks. When does it happen?

When does the change take place and you look and feel right? All these teenage stories seem to make out there's lots to look forward to. When? I look awful. No wonder Damien hates me.

There was no note on my desk at lunchtime today but there's one girl in the class who I'm sure sent it. She keeps looking at me really oddly. Her name is Patrice. I always thought that was French for Patrick. She stares a lot.

'Why don't we go and see if Thérèse is all right?' Clara suggests on the way home.

'How do you know where she lives?'

'Easy. The travellers who come to the school usually camp on the main road out of Cork. Let's dump our sacks and grab a bite and take a walk.'

Clara is amazing. I have known her for two school days and it's as if we've known each other for ever. She's fourteen, a year older than some of us in the class. She spent a long time in hospital when she was ten and missed out on school. I don't know what was wrong with her, but I wonder if that's why she's fat. Her mother and father looked normal enough when I saw them in their garden yesterday. Clara is an only child.

I can't imagine life without Ed. That's stupid. Here I am, living without him, for the time being.

Dropping my bag and taking a slice of still warm fruit cake, I go to the end of the road to wait for Clara. Luckily she's already there. The walk takes for ever. The road out of Cork leads us past loads of old buildings which are falling down.

'It's been a bad time for the city,' Clara explains. 'For

a while business was booming; now companies are pulling out and people are leaving.'

I understand how it feels to leave. I hadn't really thought about all the people who've had to move away because the jobs don't exist any more.

Clara's voice is amazing. She ought to be an actress. I suggest it. Her laugh is so loud that I feel I could easily be blown under a bus.

'What, with a figure like mine to take care of?'

'Diet,' I say, knowing that I just might be treading on very shaky ground. I would never have dared to say anything like that to Posie, but although I know I might lose Clara as soon as I've found her, it seems worth a try.

'Vanessa, I'm one of the lucky ones.' I look at her. Clara, lucky. I'd die if I were as fat as she is.

'I had leukemia. I'm still on medication. You should have seen me a couple of years ago. I was bald then as well. Three of the kids I was in hospital with are dead. I'm not going to die. In fact they think I'll be fine. One day, when the drugs are finished, I'll diet. And maybe then I'll be an actress.'

I feel awkward and shy. She claps me on the back and I almost fall under the wheels of a passing lorry.

'Here we are,' she announces.

So this is a gypsy camp.

Thirteen

I didn't want to discuss it when I got home and now I don't want to discuss it as it wriggles around in my brain. I feel like burning the memory out. How can one person make enemies so quickly? That one person being me. I've held the grave pebble so hard in my hand that there's a bruise beginning to show in my palm. Dad always told us to face up to things but I don't want to face up to the yells and the mud and the stones being thrown. I don't want to remember the dog snarling and jumping on to Clara. Or the shouts of anger in the hospital, all the hostility.

Her poor face. Clara's poor face.

We hitched to the hospital. Can you believe it, I'm thirteen and I have never stuck my thumb up to a car before! Clara didn't seem that bothered, once she was over the shock. I'd given her my new Indian scarf to stop the bleeding. She was shaking quite a lot in the car, but once we arrived at the emergency department, she was fine. Luckily I had money in my pocket, left over from this afternoon when Thérèse didn't come with us to the burger place. At least I was able to ring home.

'I'll be there at once,' mum said. 'I'll go and let Clara's parents know. Give me the address.'

I can't recall all these new things, phone numbers, names of classes, Irish rivers. How did I know what the number of the house was? So I described what it looks like and hoped for the best.

The hospital is huge and everyone is unbelievably friendly. I seem to be filling my nose with antiseptic these days, what with Puss first and now Clara. She was welcomed like an old friend by the girl at the reception desk.

'Don't forget I spend a lot of time coming in and out of here,' she explained. Poor Clara, I'm surprised she can smell anything else but that clinging hospital smell.

'We'll have her back in a little while. Could you ring her parents?' The nurse asked. 'That will keep you occupied. Stop worrying. Underneath all that blood and mud is a scratch, I promise.' The nurse gave me a hug.

'You're fine, aren't you, Clara?' The nurse asked, turning to Clara who looked as if she'd been attacked by a pack of wolves. Her hair was spiked with dirt and her face swollen around the bite on her cheek.

'Of course I am. The poor dog probably has indigestion after the chunk he tried to nibble from me. Stop looking so tragic, Vanessa. Meet Penny, she was a junior when I first started coming here; now look at her, Night Sister.'

After shaking my hand, Penny whisked Clara off into a curtained cubicle; it was then I made my phone call.

The waiting area is a bit like a hotel lounge. I almost bought a bar of chocolate but opted for an apple. The spots are even worse today and my jeans are far too tight. Then, sitting down, I waited.

'Go on, get off with you. Meddling, always meddling and poking fun,' the old man had yelled at us. We'd only just arrived at the camp site; there were four caravans parked.

'School project, I suppose. You pay to get into a zoo, you can pay to see us.' He'd started to pick up stones and was joined by three or four boys. The ground was a mire, all the recent rain had turned the whole area into a filthy swamp. I slipped but Clara fell. The old man's dog, some sort of Alsatian cross-breed, broke out of the caravan as the old man was getting in; the dog was snarling and agitated as he charged straight at us. He caught hold of Clara. I kicked him. I didn't want to but there was no other way to get him off. We didn't wait, just ran back to the main road and that's when I saw all the blood on Clara's face.

Asking why is stupid. The old man seemed more frightened than angry.

There was rubbish piled all around, bits of cars, saturated cardboard boxes. Suddenly I had this awful feeling that there was something terribly wrong with Thérèse. It felt so cold and damp with the cars and lorries rushing past, splashing water. No purple and pink flowers for Thérèse.

The time drags when you're waiting. I picked up a leaflet about AIDS and got depressed. Who will I be able to sleep with when I'm ready? How will I know if he's got AIDS? What's the point in worrying about it? But it is a thought. Anyway, at the rate my body isn't developing no boy will want anything to do with me. Then I picked up a newspaper, *The Cork Examiner* farming section. Looking at the pictures of cows and sheep I thought of all the meals they'd inadvertently

43

attended. It's a pity meat tastes so good. The next magazine was *Nursing Monthly*, which had gross pictures of a man's ulcerated leg.

Why does everything have to be so horrible? But the truth was there was something far more horrible about to happen.

Fourteen

As I was sitting there worrying about lambs, ulcers and AIDS, I didn't hear the double doors leading into the reception area being opened. One minute I was thinking about the old man and the next, there he was, in front of me, with Thérèse.

'Thérèse!' I said, jumping up. 'Are you all right?' The old man was standing awkwardly to one side, holding his hat in his hands, his head bent down. Thérèse looked exhausted, still wearing the clothes that I'd seen her in the day before. But it was her eyes which startled me. They had big, dark circles under them.

'No. Yes. Are you hurt? Grandy's dog didn't mean it. Is the girl you were with badly injured? I was just getting out of bed to come and see you when Whisky escaped. He's not normally a bad dog but all the shouting and upset must have done it.'

Poor Thérèse was in tears. I tried to make a joke of it by saying the dog was well named. Obviously he must have been drinking to have been in such a wild mood. Thérèse's grandfather remained still. It was my turn to feel ashamed. I extended my hand.

'I'm Vanessa. I'm sorry we upset you. It was thoughtless. I'm sorry.' And then the lump appeared and the tell-tale catch in my voice, my personal space between anger and sadness.

'Can I get you a cup of coffee or something while we wait for Clara?' I asked tentatively.

Then it all happened so fast. Clara's parents, who

looked ordinary enough in their front garden, arrived. Mother was with them. She was in true dramatic form. Gush, rush, flow.

'Nessie, dahling, are you all right?' They all totally ignored the old man who had moved towards them.

'Where's Clara?' Mrs Farrell, Clara's mother demanded? 'I want to see my daughter.' She stood there, eyes bulging, all wrapped up in a fur coat, with gloves on and high boots. The difference between her, cosy and protected and the grandfather and Thérèse, standing there silently, made me angry.

The pleasant receptionist joined us and tried to calm Mrs Farrell down; by this time was she calling for the police, her solicitor, someone in authority. I wanted to shout at her and mum that Clara was fine, that she'd had a big fright but that she was not dying, not this time. Suddenly I wanted a mother who doesn't cry all the time. I wanted someone solid who can calm chaos.

Mother's face is a marvellous machine. She can make her nostrils wider when she's carried away by another scene from any of her own one act plays. Without saying a word to Thérèse, she pulled me towards her as if I was about to be attacked or something. I knew what she was up to. She was putting a real distance between me and those she regarded as beneath us. As she would say, not quite 'the thing.' Without knowing anything about the situation, she was busily interfering. But she'd had time to brush her hair, and sure enough, her blusher was strategically placed on each high cheek bone. What a fraud!

And then Clara appeared. Thérèse was sitting in a corner, but as soon as she saw Clara, she began to get up. Mrs Farrell stepped in between them. It was like a very bad film.

'Don't you touch my daughter!' she spat out angrily.

I could feel my mouth fall open. Clara, with a big plaster on her cheek, looked ridiculous as her mouth sagged wide. Without any nonsense Clara ignored her mother, in fact, barged straight past her.

'Hi, I'm Clara. I've already met your dog. Do you know something, you missed out on a bloody good burger this afternoon. How about next week, that is unless you're another veggie freak like my new-found friend here?' She said all this with a massive grin at Thérèse and me.

There she was, a few hours ago half terrified, bleeding and frightened and now back to her bouncing form. It must have something to do with all she's had to put up with. I'm not that strong but I'm learning.

Clara's dad was helpless. He didn't seem to be a part of my mother's dramatics or his wife's anger. It must be very confusing being married. You're meant to feel the same way but can't because you're two completely different people. I'm convinced Mr Farrell would have spoken to the old man and Thérèse if he had been allowed, but just like my mother grabbing at me, his pushy, over-dressed wife was hanging on to his arm.

Forget it Mum and Mrs Farrell. If being socially acceptable turns me into someone like you two - I absolutely refuse to grow up.

Fifteen

As I sit here in my bedroom, I wonder what the person who slept in it before was like. It is still decorated for someone very small. Bambi and Thumper leap across the wallpaper with big grins. I could do with a friend right now.

I'm so confused. I've been to school three times. Day one, bad, the note; day two, disaster, Clara; day three ... what can I say about day three? Damien brushed past me as I sat in the classroom at lunchtime. There was no Clara. She's at home after yesterday's fiasco. No Thérèse. No nothing. But then Patrice came over to me.

'Hi, I'm Patrice,' she began.

'I know who you are,' I replied.

'Have you seen your skirt?' Her voice is hardly above a whisper.

I freeze. Oh God! What is it? What is on my skirt?

'Well,' she begins, 'it's red and I'd say you've had a bit of a leak.'

No one else is around, no one else to witness my shame. I pick up my sack and there at the bottom, along with the note from the first day, is the sanitary towel that Sorcha had given me on the plane. I want to say something, a word to let Patrice know how sorry I am to have misjudged her.

'You're a real friend,' I say, as I run out of the room down the corridor to the girls' cloakroom.

It is absolutely silent in the toilet. That's unusual.

Normally there are girls hanging around, talking. In my heart I know there cannot be anything but still, shaking, I roll down my pants. I feel so afraid. There is nothing there, but gradually I hear whispering, giggling, a snorted laugh from someone. I check the back of my skirt. There's an ugly red smear there, still damp. Ink of some sort, probably the inside of a felt-tip pen that had been left on my chair. The stain is ugly, and outside I can hear the girls chanting, 'Come out, Lochy, Lochness Monster.'

How did they know, how did they know that stupid nickname? They were all there, Patrice's friends, Patrice too, leering, smiling and laughing at me. One of them looked a bit embarrassed. It must be hard to have Patrice as a friend. And that's when it dawned on me. I don't have anyone. Well, at least I don't have to pretend that I agree with something I know is wrong and cruel. Suddenly, feeling ridiculously happy, I remembered the times when I would agree with Posie, just so that we would stay as friends. I didn't want to get on the bad side of her. I cannot explain my excitement at that little understanding.

'Stupid cow!' one of the girls yelled. I'd never seen her before. She looked ordinary enough. I was taller than any of them.

'Don't you like cows?' I asked. 'I think they're beautiful animals.'

Patrice moved towards me as if she was about to push me. I was afraid of that. I didn't want to be touched by any of them. Holding my bag in front of me, I got past them, back into the corridor. One of them called after me, 'Look what's happened to high and mighty.'

There were boys hunting through their lockers for football boots, girls leaning against the wall, talking. I could feel all those eyes on me, on my skirt.

It's September the fifth. I am Vanessa Carter. I hate where I live. I hate that school, but something inside me keeps telling me not to be beaten. Patrice and her gang are rotten. I am not.

Sixteen

Ed will be here in five weeks time. He sounded very miserable on the phone when I rang this evening. I didn't tell him why I was ringing or about the girls at school - he's obviously got enough problems of his own. What's the point in announcing over the wires under the sea that our mother has sacrificed the pair of us? She, of course, has never been happier. I didn't tell her either. I'm convinced that even if I had had my first period it wouldn't impress her very much. She's working on lectures in the study. Study ! I ask you. She didn't need to think about a study when dad was around. Now it's all big books with unpronounceable names and telephone conversations with people who sound as if they've eaten three dozen cherries and can only just open their mouths because they've forgotten to swallow them.

I tried to see Clara but her mother wouldn't let me in. She said Clara was jaded (her word, not mine). She also said that after my silly escapade (her word again), Clara was going to need a lot of rest. Clara looked as fit as one of Puss's fleas when she waved from the car last night after having the stitches put in. My mother gave me one of her little 'talks' and suggested I find someone more suitable than Thérèse. I hardly know Thérèse, but I do know that I like her. I even thought about walking down to see her but the truth is, I'm not brave enough.

Great, here I am, the new independent me, who

doesn't go and apologise for the disgusting behaviour of my mother and Clara's stuck up parents. If the way they think and the way they behave is what mother calls middle-class she can keep it to herself. At the moment being in class Breandán is sufficient.

I tried ringing Sorcha's number. No reply. Even if I'd got through to her, I wasn't going to let her know about school, but I wanted to make sure that she hadn't forgotten about Aideen coming over at the weekend. I hope she comes. Sorcha looks beautiful. Much more than that, I feel close to her. If Aideen is a tiny bit like her then I might have one friend in among the three million who live on this island.

Just as I put the phone down I noticed that Puss had discovered a brand new place to christen, mother's sheepskin rug. It belongs on the back of the sheep who owns it but I knew that she wouldn't understand Puss's disgust at having dead animals lying around the house. (I also know that that wasn't his prime motive. He's quite a gatherer of dead animals himself, pigeons mainly. He presents them to me, neatly beheaded. Revolting!)

I tried washing the rug with disinfectant. If you've ever washed sheepskin, white sheepskin, with disinfectant, you will know that it changes to a disgusting shade of brown. In a panic I then slooshed on some bleach, only making matters far worse. I could hear mother typing away in the distance and did the only reasonable thing. I rolled the rug up neatly and put it into a plastic bag.

I have tried talking to my mother about plastic and packaging and waste and ozone-gobbling sprays. She honestly doesn't believe that the world is dying. She said I was a 'faddist', whatever that is. Anyway, just as I was pushing the remains of the dead sheep into the bin, she came to the back door. Puss's scratching and miaowing was a bit of a give away.

'Dinner, Ness. What are you doing, darling? Whatever is that?' She didn't so much see it as smell it. In fact, if she'd walked through the hall, she would probably have been knocked out by the combined bleach/disinfectant smells. Potent. Anyway, tottering over to see, in high heels, she dragged the bag out of the bin. She has taken to wearing designer suits. Suits, two pieces, like royalty, with gold buttons and braid. Not saying a word, she dropped *it* distastefully back into the bin.

When my mother doesn't say anything you know that what is being left unsaid is dangerous. I followed her back into the kitchen. In the short time we have owned this house she has had the unit doors removed and replaced with mahogany fronts. I told her about hard woods. I explained that anything had to be better than a tree which takes ages to grow and seconds to cut into stupid cupboards in a stupid kitchen. She didn't listen. Well, she did. She ordered a mahogany kitchen table to complete the ensemble. Spite. It's all spite.

I bought her a book for her birthday about the rain forests. It's still unread. I know because I stuck a book-mark in page twenty-nine; it was still there the other day, I checked ...

'You destroyed that rug on purpose.' What could I say? 'You didn't like it, so you ruined it. What is all this nonsense about dead animals, Vanessa? You are becoming obsessed with death. You need a

53

psychiatrist.'

Still silent, I watched her and wondered if dad knew that he had married a tyrant.

'Do you know how difficult you're making life for Mrs Dineen? You won't eat this, you won't eat that. You're a carnivore.' She spelt it out, C.A.R.N.I.V.O.R.E.

I was going to tell her that I and the rest of humanity are omnivores, that we have a choice, but I don't think that would have been too well received. It was while I was thinking this that I watched, fascinated, as her hand went up and came down, hitting me on the side of the head.

'Take that superior look off your face,' she yelled.

The look's gone. I've gone. I'm upstairs with Thumper and Co. It's already eleven. I have a banana left over from lunch and tap water.

Tomorrow is Thursday. I am going to run away.

Seventeen

It's just come to me on this sunny autumn morning! I did start off being a vegetarian as a bit of a punishment for mum. I wanted something for me, something that I could do on my own, my own choice I suppose. Plus, mum has always prided herself on the way she can cook. Dinner parties a few years ago were a real event. There would be beautiful frilled lamb dishes, baby potatoes and shiny carrots. The puddings were works of art, cream and melted chocolate. The smells in the kitchen would bring Ed and me down the stairs and, more often than not, dad would be in the kitchen already, hugging mum. She would be standing there looking happy, wearing the big apron dad gave her, smiling, always smiling. Maybe I did originally think I'd get her attention by refusing her meals, but that can't be it now because she's not cooking any more. As she said last night, Mrs Dineen is the cook. I really like Mrs Dineen and I know that I'm not trying to get at her. Anyway, Mrs Dineen told me that she'd never had so much fun trying to find new recipes that will keep me fit and happy. Fat and unhappy would more than cover the reality.

Lying on the floor in the hall (which smells like a very badly kept public convenience at the moment) was a letter for me. I'd written off for some information about blood sports, hare coursing in particular. It seems that hare coursing is almost acceptable in some areas here. The pictures are horrific. I don't want to become a fanatic, burning down shops and the like when I don't agree with certain activities, but I do want to know more about what's going on in the world. I don't think I'm doing all this to be awkward.

For breakfast I have gorged myself on bread and butter, homemade jam and freshly squeezed juice. I have an ache in the pit of my stomach which could be from over-eating or maybe it's tension. I've decided to give school one more try. I haven't anywhere else to go.

'Telephone, Vanessa.'

The gorgon is awake, if not in evidence. I wonder how she slept last night. Hang on, she's talking to me again. Adults are incredible. She's probably forgotten she gave me a whack and sent me to bed.

'Hello.'

'Hi!' It's a voice I don't recognise. Then there's a rush of words.

'This is Aideen, Sorcha's sister, remember? Vanessa, I'm sorry I haven't rung. Sorcha kept reminding me and I kept forgetting. It was the thought of going back to school, buying books and losing my uniform that did it. Don't you hate it when the holidays come to an end and you have to get up in the mornings? I loathe it.' She sounds friendly enough.

'Is it still ok then, for Saturday? You're not doing anything else are you?'

That's a joke. I might be hitching a ride to China or somewhere equally far away. 'No, nothing.' I say.

I sounded too abrupt. She's going to think I'm really stupid and that's before I've even made a whole sentence.

'Hold on!' In my head I'm screaming, don't go away.

In fact what I'm doing is picking up Puss, who's looking remarkably furry for a cat who didn't possess much of a coat a couple of weeks ago, but is also sniffing around for his missing friend, the dead sheep. Banging the front door shut, with him on the other side, I rush back.

Brrrrr ... She's gone. Aideen has rung off.

I'm wondering as I walk to school if it was the fact that it was eight forty five that made her ring off, or me!

'You look miserable.' It's Damien? 'I saw Clara yesterday. With luck she'll be back next week. Her mother's taking her to Dublin today to see some specialist or other.'

'She's not ill again, is she?' I ask frantically.

'No. She has regular check ups and her mother insists that she goes up to Dublin despite the fact that she was treated here in Cork in the first place.'

He's nice, taller than me, with an old canvas bag slung across his shoulder; it's heavily painted with rock groups. His hair is kind of crazy, long and wild. He has the most beautiful, crooked smile.

'You've met her mother!' He adds with a wink. Then he asks, 'What do you think of it so far?'

'Of what?'

'Oh! The school, Cork, Ireland, the world, the latest film, politics, underage drinking, parents. You name it. What do you think of it ?'

He's mad. He's talking to me and I don't dare tell him what I think about anything. He probably already knows about yesterday. He probably saw me, might even have been a part of the whole thing.

'It's all right, I suppose.'

'What, Vanessa? What's all right? Which bit? Not the school, surely. You know, a lot of us wouldn't mind getting to know you, but you kind of look haughty, superior, as if none of us is quite good enough for you. Clara says that's not true. She told me how you tried to stand up for Thérèse. Why don't you give some of us a chance?'

I cannot believe what I'm hearing. The sun is shining, my skirt is dry but a bit creased where I washed the pen out of it and the wool has matted. I have a huge lunch to make up for yesterday's starvation and I'm walking into school, talking to Damien Kelleher who has to be the most interesting person in my class.

'Vanessa Carter.' It's the headmaster. I know who he is from assembly. Why does he want me? Oh no! Yesterday.

'In my office, now please.'

Damien gives me another wink. Anyone else would look stupid doing that. I can face whatever is going to happen. I have a friend.

Eighteen

The headmaster's office is more of a cupboard than an important meeting place. Lists of exams, sports fixtures and newspaper cuttings are pinned on to a notice board behind his head. I am very wary of how I look, not how I'm dressed but how my face seems to the outside world. I was worrying about spots. Damien thought I was haughty. Mother thinks I'm superior. What's the headmaster going to think ?

He is not old, well, oldish, about mother's age. He has black hair and very dark eyes. The more I look at his eyes as he looks at me, the more I realise that he could stop a passing rhinoceros with that stare. He's wearing a stripy suit with a white shirt and a navy tie. He looks like a doctor, except for the eyes.

'Vanessa.' The voice is surprisingly soft, not hard as it was in the corridor. 'I heard from various sources about what happened yesterday.' I hang my head. He knows, he knows they all hate me. I am going to run away. Where ? Where can I go ? If I'd been sick, like Clara, then maybe people would feel sorry for me. But I don't feel sorry for Clara. I feel sorry for me.

'Firstly, it will not happen again. Bullying on any level is reprehensible. Be assured the matter has been dealt with. Secondly, I should like you to have a look at this report which I received the other day from your old school.'

How embarrassing! My hands are shaking as I take the typed sheets from him. It's going to be full of how I don't work, refuse to cooperate, am disruptive in class. I've heard it all before. Reading it, I cannot believe my eyes, especially the bit that maintains I am showing potential in English and History. We can forget the History now that I'm here, or maybe I'll give it another go.

'It's not easy settling into a new school, Vanessa. This is a big school and you are bound to feel a little lost for a while. Your mother rang a few moments ago. She's very concerned.'

Concerned, my eye. She hates me. Only someone who hates someone else hits out like she did last night. She starved me as well. I won't say anything. What's the point? All these so-called adults stick together. They haven't a clue what it's like, how it feels.

'We have a counsellor in the school. Her name's Mrs Morrow. Any time that you feel you need someone to talk to, go along to her room. I'll explain where it is. Leave her a note on her desk and she will be sure to see you.'

I also know about notes left on desks. Suddenly his eyes aren't stopping runaway rhinos. Eyes are so telling. His look hard when his voice is hard but they are soft now.

'I have a daughter of twelve. She and I clash quite a lot at the moment. That's the way it's meant to be. She's growing up and I keep on forgetting it, resent it, if you can understand that.'

If I open my mouth I'll yell out that I don't have a father, and that when I did we didn't argue. But what's the point?

'The clashes that I have with my daughter are nothing compared to the ones she has with her

60

mother.' I look up at him and I know he knows, that mum has told him exactly how badly we're getting on.

'People have to talk, Vanessa. Unluckily parents cannot read minds. Sometimes they attempt to read faces and receive the wrong message completely. Because you are tall for your age and your face is maturing, you can appear older, wiser even than you are.' He looks at me directly. 'Give it a try anyway, talking, not shouting. You never know, you and your mother can probably sort all this out more quickly than you think. However, work hard!' Now he's back to being brisk and business-like. 'How do you find the Italian during the Irish classes?'

'It's fine. I'm enjoying it.' I'm not. But going on about buzzing headphones and the noise in the classroom while people around me are speaking with forked tongues wrapped around unpronounceable words would seem a bit ungrateful after he's tried to be so nice. He gets up and then opens the door of his cupboard-cum-office.

'Good luck!' he says and disappears back into his box.

This new headmaster must be a nice kind dad to have. He talked about his daughter as if he knew how she was feeling. I wonder what she's like? Where she goes to school? She has a dad and I bet she doesn't even care that he cares about her.

Nineteen

I have been at school for three days now and on my fourth I am beginning to know where to go. Walking to my classroom I can see various statues. There's St Michael crushing the head of some poor, unsuspecting cloven-hooved man. I tend to identify with the underdog. St Michael looks awfully smug. The real importance of the statue is that two doors down from it, on the left, is my classroom. Stopping outside the door I can hear they are saying morning prayers, in Irish.

As I walk into the room I gulp back fear. I cannot imagine anything more terrible than all those eyes boring into you when you walk into a place. I'm saying a prayer as well that I won't bang into anything or drop my bag, that I will make it to my desk and sit down without falling off my chair. I'm convinced I'm going to have a heart attack before I'm fourteen. The way it pounds and the way my ears ring cannot be good for a body. Still, not dead and my bag safely on the floor beside me, I bless myself along with the rest of them. It's so hypocritical ! I don't believe in half the stuff I'm supposed to but at least it's familiar.

The scraping of chairs as everyone sits down really hurts my head. One good thing is that it's English first lesson. Looking through my bag, I can feel the panic again. I cannot find last night's homework. I'm sure I did it. My hands are slippery with sweat. Where is it?

And then I remember. I wasn't here for most of yesterday. Will I have to explain? Our English teacher, Mr O'Donnell, loves his subject. You can sense it as soon as he starts talking about *Romeo and Juliet* or *Jane Eyre*. They are living people to him and what happens to them on a page is as real as what's happening in the class. In a few days he has made me want to understand the old English words that Shakespeare used. It's all about love; the books, the songs, even the poetry we're doing is about falling in and out of love. Poetry is Mr O'Donnell's passion. He has a deep voice which sings out the words; even when some of the girls are whispering and the boys making comments, he keeps reading. I like poetry too. I can't understand half of it but I love the way it rolls. I wish I knew what it meant.

'Vanessa, will you read out the essay you wrote on Monday? There are one or two people here who could do with listening to how a complete paragraph should sound.'

No, I will not read. I will not stand up to make an example of myself. He's walking towards me with my copy in his hands. He is going to give it to me. Doesn't he realise what this will do? It will make me more of an outsider than ever. For a sensitive man he's got about as much soul as a cockroach. As he hands it to me I drop it and, bending down, I bang the side of my head on the desk. I can hear sniggers. I try telepathy. Maybe he'll read my mind. No luck, he's already back at his desk, waiting patiently. All right, I'll read, but not standing up; my legs won't support me.

Everything is in slow motion. My head is aching from fear and from the bash I've given my poor skull.

My hands are like two big feet that don't know how to curl. I try to read out the title. 'School Holidays'. Normally I would think what a stupid waste of time to write an essay on such a boring subject, but I really tried because it was the first thing I had written for Mr O'Donnell.

My brain isn't working quickly enough and my voice keeps on fading. They are all watching me, fascinated. I can feel moisture gathering under my arms and in between what will one day, hopefully, be my breasts. I can't hear myself and then suddenly, as if someone has turned up the volume, I hear my voice, very English, very clipped, very different. I hate my mother more than anything in the whole world for having done this to me. And I even hate my father because if he hadn't smoked he wouldn't have had a stroke and he certainly would not have died. How many times did I tell them. No one listens, not to young people. Then I feel in my pocket for the pebble. It's there. I try to imagine a curtain all around me and I finish reading my ridiculous little essay.

Twenty

It's eleven o'clock. English, German and Maths are out of the way. The classroom is emptying because we have to return to our own room, the one St Michael and his goaty friend are guarding. I had another look at the statue on the way to Maths. It's really wrong the way the person who made it has given the devil figure a very dark skin, as if that were all part of being the wrong-doer. I might even mention it in religion class. I have to drop off my books and collect what I need for break time. No one has spoken to me since this morning. Do I exist?

'Right, Miss Bronte!' I look round. It's Damien. 'Now you can meet the gang. Come on, stop looking so tragic. You'll give us all a pain and we haven't even been into the biology lab yet to look at the rat on offer for dissection!'

I can feel myself smiling. 'Do I look that bad?' I ask.

'No. You look fine but you always seem as if you're going to burst into tears any minute.'

I'd like to explain to him that I have absolutely no control over my face, but don't bother. He walks very quickly and talks even faster, as if there isn't enough time. It's quite difficult understanding him. All the words are rushed together. Pushing past people standing in the doorway, he slips his bag down and grabs Catherine, the girl I said looked nice when I saw her on the first day.

'Catherine, you've met Vanessa. Meet her again. She's a slow starter!'

'Hi again!' she says. 'That essay was good. Isn't it the pits when you have to read out loud? I don't know how you did it. I always go weak at the knees.'

'It's worse than that,' I reply. 'It's as if you're on display for the whole world to have a good laugh. If I ever teach, which I won't, but if I do, I'll never ask my students to read out loud or make them seem better than anyone else.'

There's a group of five: Damien, Catherine, Kieran, Grace and Enda. Not one of them is looking at me strangely. They're all agreeing with me. Then Catherine mentions it ... yesterday.

'We all know what Patrice and her cronies did, Vanessa. It was bloody stupid, if you'll excuse the pun. You might have noticed that they're not in today. Rumour has it that they've been suspended until next week. I promise you she won't be any problem to you when she gets back. None of us can stand her, so stick with us and you'll be fine.'

Day four and Catherine reckons I'm going to be all right. Shall I abandon pessimism for hope?

Damien's father is an electrical engineer. He works in a place called Ballincollig. Damien is the oldest of nine children. Nine! That seems obscene to me. According to Damien on the way home, it's a bit noisy in his house! He wanted to know whether I'd like to come over on Friday evening. I would love to but will the dragon lady let me? He's easy to talk to. In fact I don't have to talk at all because he natters away. I used to imagine what it would be like, walking along with a boy, chatting, and here I am, doing just that and it's nothing extraordinary apart from the fact that I don't want to say anything that will make me sound stupid. He doesn't seem to be bothered. I mutter something. He answers. We say goodbye.

Walking up the path into the garden, I feel peaceful. Not for long. Help! What is it now? There she is, mother, crying. Here we go again.

Twenty-one

It can only be Puss. That would somehow fit in with
everything else. I'm not even going to run up the
driveway or look at his corner. I'm not going to do
anything. I'm not going to cry either. She hated the cat
and now she's crying only because she's guilty. Good
luck to her. The headmaster thinks he knows what she's
like. Well, I know differently.

She runs up and hugs me. She smells strange, very
hot, and she's not all dressed up, just in jeans and a
sweater. I suppose she didn't want to get blood on her
good clothes. I'm still not going to say anything. She
won't understand. The house is warm. The smell of
bread and oven heat in the kitchen should make me
feel at home, but I don't. The mahogany table has a big
bunch of flowers in a crystal vase on it. Everywhere
looks bright and clean and tidy. I try to imagine
Damien's kitchen, with nine children in it. I can't.

Sitting me down (which isn't easy with my bag
weighing me over to one side) she begins.
'Vanessa, I ... ' She lets out a sigh. 'Vanessa, where can
I begin?'
You could always show me the dead cat, I think.
'I've been pretty selfish recently, Ness. I got all caught
up with the excitement and preparation of coming
here. I spoke to your headmaster this morning. I told
him about yesterday and how I lost my temper. He also

told me about the stupid trick those girls played on you. Why didn't you tell me, Nessie? I would have listened.' She pauses for breath.

'Ness, has your period started?'

I shake my head. Why does she want to know, anyway? That's my business. Now she's really crying. It's my turn, to hug her and reassure her that she's not as bad as I know she is. I have to act like I'm the mother. I'm the one with all the problems and she needs comforting.

'Vanessa, please, can we try again. I haven't thought straight for a long time. But as your headmaster explained to me, you are the one having to do all the adjusting.'

She's the one with the degrees, about to start lecturing et cetera. And it took a phone call with a perfect stranger to point out the obvious.

Puss is clawing at my bag, trying to get at my lunch box and hoping to find a titbit. The dead cat lives!

Mum is now sitting opposite me drinking coffee and tumbling out apologies. I want to believe her, but I don't trust her anymore.

'Do you have much homework?' she asks.

'Not too much,' I reply, lying. Well, the way I see it, if we are to make some vain attempt at reconciliation, I'd better put in a bit of an effort. Plus I'm ridiculously happy that the mangey fur ball is digging his claws into my knees trying to get me to stroke him.

'How would you like to go to the hairdresser first, then on to do a bit of shopping? I know they stay open late on a Thursday. After that we could eat out.'

Hang on, I thought, this is all about me.

'No thanks, mum. I like my hair the way it is.' I lie

again.

I'm watching her reaction. She is consciously not saying anything.

'What I would really like to do is go and see Thérèse, to make sure that she's getting better. And, if she's all right, take her with us for something to eat, that is if her mother will let her.'

Mum has developed a little twitch in her right eye; when something troubles her it moves. There it goes again.

'Fine,' she says.

Getting changed out of my uniform, I wonder what Thérèse's mother is going to be like. Life is beginning to look quite interesting.

Twenty-two

Driving down to the gypsy camp takes about two minutes. Oh, but it would be lovely to be able to drive. I would be free then. Whenever anything went wrong I could climb into my car and take off, and think. I could go to the beach, listen to the waves. I could give people lifts when they are standing at bus stops in the rain. I loathe it when someone you know drives past while you're silently drowning waiting for a bus you know you've missed, or they've forgotten to send out.

Mum is still in jeans and a jersey with runners on her feet and no make-up on her face. Her short hair has grown a bit. She looks softer. I'm dressed in jeans too and they feel tight. I might even ask her later if that's what happens when you're growing up: you feel fat all the time. She never looks fat or says she feels her clothes are too tight. I won't bother asking her.

Knocking on the old man's caravan door I warn mum about Whisky. She produces a stick from behind her back. I hadn't noticed her getting it out of the car but then I was too busy looking at the mess all around me. It's so dirty. No wonder people don't want travellers on their doorstep. I'm going to say something to Thérèse about it.

The old man opens the door and there's no evidence of his hound. That makes me feel a little easier. He takes us over to Thérèse's caravan and we walk into a wonderland of pottery and glass. It feels damp, even though there's a gas fire burning. Mum introduces herself to Thérèse's mother who looks even paler than Thérèse.

'Would it be possible, then?' mum asks. 'I'll make sure I have her back to you around nine o'clock. That's not too late, is it?'

Thérèse is beaming. She's much prettier than me. She has black hair and green eyes. I'd call that positive colouring. I'm a muddy mousehead and I haven't yet found the right word to describe my eyes. Mum says they're hazel; she's biased. When the nondescript look comes in I'll be a fashion leader!

Mrs McDermott seems unsure. We look pleadingly at her. She looks from me, to mum, to Thérèse. We're smiling, and then she agrees.

I can feel myself relaxing as we get back into the car. Thérèse sits in the back seat and I begin to find out how she is. She hasn't been to school since the first day.

'It's nothing, really. I get these colds. They go to my chest and eventually they go away again.'

'Have you seen the doctor?' mum asks. You can tell from the tone of her voice that she doesn't approve.

'Yes. He gave me an antibiotic but mum doesn't like me to take too much medicine.'

There it goes, the twitch. I can feel her thinking. Not suitable company. A child whose mother isn't into stuffing her offspring with drugs! How very irresponsible!

After a few moments mum has us seated in the Indian restaurant. It's empty. No wonder she didn't mind bringing Thérèse out. She knows that no one eats here until much later. But I won't say anything.

Thérèse is in a different skirt and jersey. They look as bad as the others she wore on that first day. Anyway, the food's good and Thérèse is eating everything in sight, despite the fact that she's never been in a restaurant before, never mind an Indian one with the famous long-haired waiter.

He greeted me like an old friend and explained that today he had some wonderful mushrooms. Maybe they're magic mushrooms which will turn my mother into someone I can talk to and turn Thérèse into a long lost heiress. I think I've just had a revelation, and that's before eating the mushrooms. (If having a brilliant idea, like a blinding flash out of nowhere, is a revelation, that's what I've had.) I'm not going to mention it yet. I think it might need a bit of planning. Suddenly I'm so happy! Funny old business this living, either up or down. But it can be interesting.

Twenty-three

After dinner Thérèse came back to the house. I
suggested she have a hot bath and try on some of the
gear that I've outgrown. I know that suggesting a bath
sounds terrible, but, as she said, they can only wash at
the sink in their caravan. That must be pretty cold. No
wonder she has a permanent chest infection. When you
read what some people have to say about gypsies! They
make out the travelling people are millionaires. Thérèse
and her mother and grandfather definitely don't fit into
that category. She says she doesn't mind the word
gypsy at all, that it makes her feel part of a really old
tradition; that must be a nice feeling. I'm Vanessa
Carter, vegetarian and that's about it.

She liked everything I gave her and, what is more,
she didn't make me feel as if I were some awful Lady
Bountiful doling out stuff to the poor. She was so
excited.
'Are you sure, Ness? Those sweat shirts were very
expensive ... '
'And too small,' I interrupted.
Thérèse looked good now, dressed in faded denims,
a black sweat shirt and a pair of flat ballet shoes which I
had always hated but which look really good on her.
She asked if she could try some of my make-up. I use a
bit of lip gloss now and then and tinted moisturiser
when I'm feeling really into it but, to be perfectly
honest, looking in the mirror for any length of time

depresses me. I look like one of those 'before' advertisements, you know, before you've used the magic cream, lotion, powder. Even if I were to use them, I'd still look like a before version! Mum gave me a load of gunk for my thirteenth birthday. It's still sitting there in all its boxes, gathering dust and Puss fur. He likes sniffing at it. Probably thinks it's more food.

Thérèse put on a bit of mascara. It looked great.

'We'll be moving off soon,' Thérèse said. 'Sometimes I wonder what it would be like to stay in one place. Ma and grandy enjoy a lot of it. They meet up with old friends, families they've known for years. They look forward to the next market or fair but ... ' She looked sad as her voice trailed off. I began to feel excited, not because she was sad, but because she was not all that happy about leaping around the countryside. I didn't say anything, but like one of my magic mushrooms, an idea was growing in my head.

'Why is everywhere so filthy?' I know I shouldn't be too direct, but Thérèse is so easy going. Sitting opposite me, dressed in my clothes, she looked as if a small piece of me had slipped out to join me in my room.

'When *you* finish with a tin or packet, what do you do with it?' She asked.

'Put it in the bin,' I replied.

'Where are the bins where we park?' She had me. But they could shove some of the rubbish into bags, toss it into one of those big bins at a supermarket or something. Also, who says they have to keep travelling. How about staying in one place where there are bins and bathrooms? I suggested all this to her, as a thought, a chewable suggestion. Suddenly, meek and mild

Thérèse of pale face and sad eyes flashed back at me.

'We have a right to choose. If travelling's the way we've lived for centuries, who has given outsiders the right to tell us we are wrong? What's the difference between that inheritance and someone who lives in a castle passing it on to the next generation?'

'The mess! Where you're living isn't a camp site. It's squeezed on to the side of a main road. That's not an inheritance. It's a liability. It's dirty and it's dangerous and you are perpetually ill because of it.'

I was actually feeling a little bit afraid as I plunged headlong into the argument. But I wanted to know. Thérèse, who'd curled herself up on the bed, hugging one of my bears, suddenly chucked it down and looked as if she was going to storm out.

'Vanessa, supermarket managers don't want the likes of us in their car parks. God forbid if we enter their shops. We might touch a customer. Don't you see, once there was loads of room: the roads were built long after we started roaming. Camp fires were lit in the past, food was cooked, rubbish was burnt or washed cleanly away by the rain. There were good and bad among us, but because we are seen as being different, every small thing gets noticed. All the old metal, the mess as you call it, is like a scrapyard to my grandfather. That was his business. He's getting old and there's no one around to help. Thanks to my father, there will be no grandson.'

She sounded bitter. And yet her eyes didn't look angry. They just looked tired.

'I have a feeling that eventually my mother will stop travelling. She's not used to anything else, but she's weary. She's not cut out for the life in some ways, not on her own. Do you know something - she's not even thirty yet and already she looks ten years older.'

What could I say? I understood the supermarket manager's point of view. Why should his car park, built for customers, be turned into a sewer? Why should those caravans, with rubbish piling up, be allowed to park just any old where. But I understood what Thérèse was saying too. Surely there's a compromise in there somewhere?

We were all very quiet in the car taking Thérèse back. Mum was more silent than usual because Puss was found sleeping in her room. I looked at her as she drove along, all concealed indignation, all puffed up because she'd taken Thérèse out for the evening. My mother, who rarely looks any age, just smart and snappy. Both mothers without husbands. Maybe it's marriage that messes everything up.

'Something will have to be done about that animal,' she said, pulling away from the camp. 'He's a health hazard.'

The vet insisted he was a Purrfect specimen. Peter Fairhead is such a jerk.

Twenty-four

It was totally silent in the house when we got back. Doing my homework wasn't too bad because at school when I was supposed to be doing Italian during Irish, I managed to clear Maths and Geography instead. It isn't going to work, this studying a language on my own. It sounds altogether far too much effort for my liking. And why was the stupid idea thought up in the first place? I was conceived in Italy, on their second honeymoon, or something equally revolting.

The telephone kept on ringing and ringing. Leaping down the stairs into the hall, I half imagined it was Damien. Silly thought. I picked up the receiver.

'Hello.' It was Uncle Tony. He sounded worried, wanted to speak to mum urgently. I felt it again, that awful dread that something terrible was about to happen, that it had happened already and that we were the last to know.

'Is Ed all right?' I asked. He said yes, but I could feel from his voice that he meant no.

I banged on the study door and then barged in. It wasn't locked. I couldn't believe what I saw. There was Peter Fairhead with his arm round mum, who was sitting at her desk looking up at him. She looked so happy. I hadn't heard him knock at the front door, or ring the bell.

Did she let him sneak in so that I wouldn't know? I wanted to yell *traitor*, to shout loud enough for Uncle

Tony to hear.

'It's Uncle Tony on the phone. Something's wrong,' was all I could come out with.

Ed has run away. I'm not worried. He's almost eighteen. He'll arrive today or tomorrow. Mum seems to think he's already living in a cardboard box in London. What she doesn't appreciate is that he's running to her and away from Tony, and the crying baby and Ben, who can be a pain in the neck when he doesn't get his own way. I'm definitely not worried about Ed. But I am worried about her, mum. Peter's old enough to be her father.

She was too busy being dramatic to listen to me, so I left her flapping and came back upstairs. I have stolen frozen yogurt from the fridge. It's beginning to melt. I've also nicked three apples and a carton of juice, just in case I get hungry during the night. I can't sleep.

Opening the curtains on to the garden I can see wisps of trees. Somewhere out there, my brave, misunderstood cat is hunting. He's probably remembering all his glory days, when he could chase every she cat in town. Trust stupid Peter to put an end to that - although Puss does look much healthier now. Maybe there's a cat version of AIDS and he has been saved.

I wonder what Ed will make of this place when, or if, he gets here. Why he would want to live in a cardboard box is a mystery to me. I've seen pictures of people who actually do it. They can't afford to rent a place, so they sleep rough. Then, when they try to get a job, they look rough, so they don't get the job.

Please, God, let Ed turn up tomorrow.

Twenty-five

Day five. It's Friday. A whole week, my first week, and it's almost over. I suppose there is one thing I cannot say about it, boring! No, events have been dripping off the calendar like fat from sausages.

'Now, class Breandán!' It's Mr Harcourt, social studies teacher. 'I think for the next month you should adopt your own project. Whether it's the elderly confined in understaffed geriatric wards, the sick, the infirm with little or no access to assistance or the unemployed. I want you to read and investigate. By investigate ... ' He stops. 'Enda,' he says sharply.

Enda is having a whispered talk with Damien.

'Yes, Enda, is there something you wish to share with the class?'

This is only our second social studies session. Mr Harcourt is very young, very earnest. He's also really nervous. I feel sorry for him. Patrice, in the first class, had wanted to know if sex education was to be a part of social studies. Mr Harcourt blushed and said he would be dealing with *that* later in the year. If only he'd just come straight back at her with something funny he'd be a lot more comfortable now. I can see him raking around the desks with his eyes. It's ok, I'm thinking for him. She's not here today. She won't be back until next week. We both have time to prepare for her.

'Well, Enda?' he questions.

'I suggested to Damien that we study the influence of

the hamburger on the young.'

Enda has long curly hair. It is quite possible that she suggested just that to Damien. They make a lovely couple. Damien didn't walk to school with me today. I was late, so I suppose that didn't help. It's a miracle that I'm here at all. I don't think I slept last night. Then at lunchtime I went out early to find Thérèse. We ate our sandwiches in the dining area. It's getting a bit cold to sit outside.

Damien's probably forgotten that I was meant to be going to his house tonight. To think that I thought I had everything sorted out! Thérèse, me, Damien. Nothing stays the same for very long. I'm not even asking to be happy, just normal.

Mr Harcourt is still studying Enda, as if trying to decide whether or not he is yet again being made to appear a fool. Believing she's serious he agrees that the fast food phenomenon, as he calls it, will be a more than worthy study. Teachers are so thick at times. Mr Harcourt looks young but he's already adopted the hurt teacher look.

I'd love to do something about meat and why we only think about eating dead things. Then he pounces on me.

'Vanessa, what are your thoughts on the hamburger?'

Even as I open my mouth I know that I'm going to dig a hole so deep it will take an excavator to pull me out.

'I hate meat. I hate the idea of something having to die for me to live. I hate ... ' I'm going on and on, getting more emotional and wild in my accusations. Help! I can feel all those eyes again. They loathe me. Why did I start? I could have pretended that the hamburger is the best thing to happen to young and old alike.

A boy called Andrew something or other - the class brain and probably going to be moved to the top group - is positively leaping up and down, with his hand flapping like a palm tree.

'All I can say about her,' he's pointing at me, 'and her bleeding heart routine about poor fluffy wuffy creatures is, has she ever considered where the milk she pours on her oh so clean cornflakes comes from? Where the yogurt she spoons into her pretty unbloodied mouth comes from?'

I can feel myself growing redder and redder. I tried to french plait my hair this morning and it's all falling out, spiking the sides of my face.

'She lives off the back of the meat industry. She relies on people like my father to do the killing for her.'

I should have known it! I'm sitting in a classroom full of farm owners' progeny. Cows and sheep are pounds and pence to them. They are their inheritance. I want to die. That would be so much easier than this. Then mum could marry Peter. Ed could live in his cardboard box in London and Puss could sit on my grave, dreaming of mice.

'Well, Vanessa?' It's Mr Harcourt again. He looks as if he's a big fat salmon someone has let off the hook. I would like to tell him I am extremely unwell. I would also like not to have Andrew pinhead smiling victoriously across from me. I want him eaten by a lion. And then it comes to me. Inspiration.

'Vegetarians do not require milk. They have soya. We do not have to kill sheep for their wool. That is a gift from them to us.' There's a snort of laughter; it did sound a bit pathetic. 'Plastic is as good as leather. Nothing living has to die to give it to us.' I hope and pray that no one looks at my repulsive leather school shoes for which mum paid forty pounds. Or worse still, checked my lunch, cheese and pineapple with apricot yogurt for afters.

'To the narrow-minded,' I say looking pointedly at Andrew, 'ours is a rather boring option but I believe the whole world should be fed on ... ' on what, somewhere in my head is a word, what is it? 'cereals!' It came to me, just before I thought of soaps. Association of ideas again.

I will always hate this speaking out loud. And I am going to have to do a lot more research into all this stuff about milk and cheese. But right now there's a round of applause, started by Damien. Andrew hasn't been eaten by a lion but he looks distinctly deflated.

What a week! What a mess!

Twenty-six

'You're quite a fire-brand behind that cool exterior. I
don't agree with you, but good luck.'

Standing beside me, with Enda holding on to his arm
is a smiling, teasing Damien. I feel weak. I'm in a state
of shock. I shouldn't have got so worked up in that
argument with Andrew. But I did. Now it's home time,
my first post school weekend. I was so busy making a
fool of myself I forgot it was the last class.

'Well, do you think a meat eating, milk drinking,
leather jacket wearing individual could join up? I'd be
interested to find out a bit more about all that stuff?'

If Damien could see the look on Enda's face as he
puts in this request I think he would decide against
mixing with a radical vegetarian. She looks as if one
more word from him, and any from me, will result in
my instant despatch to the local slaughterhouse. Enda
has one of those pouty mouths that look as if they've
just been kissed. I have never had as much as a touch
on the side of my cheek from anyone but a relative. I
wonder what it's like?

'Come on, Damien. Vanessa is obviously too deeply
engrossed in her little green world to be bothered
answering you.'

Bitch! How can someone as nice as Damien be caught
up with *her*, apart from the mouth, long curly hair, spot
free face and husky voice.

'I'm sorry. I wasn't listening properly ... '

'Well, how about this evening, when you come over?

We could have a bit of a think about the project then. ok? You are allowed to come? Did you ask your mother?'

Enda's lower lip is now jutting furiously over her top teeth. Not very attractive! Help! I don't want to hurt anyone, break up a beautiful friendship or whatever it is they have. I am flattered though. I thought he'd forgotten and he hasn't. Damien appears to be totally unaware of the uncomfortable atmosphere. While I'm forming my reply, Enda gives me a look that would by-pass the slaughterhouse and catapult me back to the middle ages to be hung, drawn and quartered.

Shoving the loose bits of hair behind my ears and trying not to sound flustered, I say, 'That's fine. I'll have to go home and change. If you give me the address we'll be over later.'

'We?' Enda asks flatly.

'Is that all right? I thought that Thérèse could come along as well. You don't mind, do you?' I am saying all this like a non-stop record, babbling. Enda is smiling at me as if I've decided to abandon any brain she might have thought I possessed.

'Of course it's all right.'

She too can experience the joys of a good, old fashioned, over-productive Irish family.' Damien hands me a piece of paper with instructions, the address and even a cartoon of his house in relation to mine, and saunters off, with Enda, like some growth, firmly attached to his arm.

Vanessa Carter, you said you simply wanted to get to know him, not to go out with him. Yes, that's true, but I would love to know how it feels to have a boyfriend, someone I had chosen and who had chosen me. I know it's ridiculous but it must be so nice, so nice to have someone special, someone who wanted to know you even though your hair is straggly and you have spots and make stupid uninformed comments about subjects you've hardly thought about. I want to talk to someone about my mother, me, my missing brother. I couldn't discuss it with Thérèse. She was totally miserable at lunchtime. Apparently the gardaí (police) had been round and told her grandfather it was time they all moved on. There had been some thefts reported by a local garage. I can't see her grandfather climbing through a skylight to steal a few tools, and the other caravans with the boys and their parents had moved off before the complaint. As awful as the yellow stone house is, at least it's stationary.

I think doing a project on outsiders would be more appropriate. Category number one, a brand new species. A Vanessa.

Twenty-seven

The hallway leading out of the school is bursting with people desperate to escape. They just want to get home and start the weekend. I'm in such a rush I accidentally knock into one of the first years. He drops his sack, spilling all his books, gym gear and a half-eaten lunch on the ground. I notice how small he is. For the so-called dominant sex, young males take an amazingly long time to grow ! Still, it was his first week too.

'How did you get on?' I ask.

'What?' He looks puzzled.

'It was your first week, wasn't it?' No doubt he's in sixth year, doing his Leaving and I've now reopened all earlier wounds inflicted on him over the past miserable years of his small life.

He smiles. Relief. He is in first year. We begin to stuff everything back into the bag.

'It's not too bad, I suppose. But I hate these.' He pulls at the grey wool trousers he's wearing.

'Good point, and I hate this.' My turn to tear at the itchy skirt.

'Vanessa, could you come here for a moment.' It's the headmaster. No doubt he heard my subversive comment about the uniform. The boy disappears into the crush and I follow the headmaster into his office.

He doesn't say anything until we've climbed into his box and firmly shut the door.

He offers me a chair and then sits down. As teachers and heads go, this one is very polite. I wonder if Uncle

Tony is as nice to his pupils. I suspect not. He's a bit set in his ways. He thinks children in school are children, not young adults. He tends to speak and want an immediate reaction. I like this new headmaster's approach.

'Did you have a chance to see Mrs Morrow, the counsellor?'

'Not yet. I will. Maybe next week,' I answer.

'In your own time. She's not going to disappear and you have a weekend ahead of you to look forward to. Any plans?'

I feel like telling him to mind his own business but shake my head.

'How was today? Better?'

I wonder if he's really interested or if he's worried I'm going to sell my story to a cheap newspaper for a lot of money, complaining about cruelty to children or something.

He wishes me a happy weekend and I dash out, leaving him in his secret teacher's world.

Thérèse is there, waiting, looking anxiously around.

'Sorry, Trass,' I apologise. We decided she needed a nickname. I said Trass sounded too much like trash but she assured me that she didn't mind a bit. As we walk along I suggest she comes with me to meet Damien and his family.

'At least you'll know eleven more people than you did this morning. Even if they do all live under one roof, with the same surname.'

She looks worried again.

'If you say what's the point one more time, I'll scream,' I warn her. 'Who knows? Even if you have to move off this time, maybe you'll come back.'

She can be very hard going.

Anyway, once I've got her to agree I feel better. I do not think Enda would be too pleased if she discovered I'd been visiting her boyfriend on my own. What's more, going back to that rotten caravan for the whole evening doesn't sound like an exciting start to the weekend.

I used to love Fridays. They were even more fun than Saturdays in some ways, planning, imagining who we were going to meet, discovering what was on at the cinema. The yellow house is quiet this Friday evening, as usual. As I get into my jeans I'm praying as hard as I can that Ed is safe. Why hasn't he rung? I hope he hasn't been kidnapped. Who'd want to kidnap Ed anyway? Mother said darkly there were a lot of strange people out there. I know that. That's why I hate reading newspapers. I simply hope all the strange people were taking a day off when Ed decided to make a run for it. When he does get here - I daren't think *if* - he's going to have to get used to a lot of changes.

Come home, Ed.

Twenty-eight

We didn't get to Damien's until well after six. I couldn't get away early because my mother insisted that someone had to be in the house in case Ed arrived. I had tried to reason with her that, if he started out yesterday afternoon, there was no way he could make it to us until late tonight, even tomorrow. It simply wasn't possible. Uncle Tony had rung again to say that Ben had found Ed's bank book. All his money had been withdrawn. Trust Ben to be on the spot with information. I'm not sure I like little kids. They look all sweet and innocent but there's something knowing about Ben.

'Mum, if you're really worried, why don't you stay here and wait for him. You don't have to go to the library.'

She got very agitated about that, said it wasn't the point, that she needed a united front. Either she's flipped again or she's reading too much history or something. Luckily (for once), Peter arrived, so I made a quick get away. Words cannot describe what I think about that man.

Mrs Dineen was cooking pancakes in the middle of my shouting match with mum. It's awful. I like her, Mrs Dineen that is, but you can't have a decent, no-holds-barred row any more, without someone looking on. I will never keep goldfish now that I know how they must feel, poor little things, objects on display, with memories that cut out after four seconds.

Trass arrived back dressed in another of the sweatshirts and jeans, with the ballet shoes in a bag. She said she didn't want to wreck them walking up the main road. If only Ed would arrive I could talk through my idea with him. But the mood that mum is in at the moment doesn't make me feel too hopeful.

If Posie were to see the house that Damien and his family live in, she'd die of shame. Looking back on it, I often wonder now how Posie and I ever became friends. I love to talk, work things out, which means I'm always putting my foot into someone else's problems. Posie enjoyed talking about people, how awful her parents were, and how horrible my mother is (I can't disagree with her there), and how untidy our house was. It all seems so long ago.

Damien's house is called Forsters, nobody knows why. It should be called Fortress because all the floors, right up to the attic, are made of concrete. It has metal doors and metal window frames. Apparently the man who built it in nineteen thirty something was a bit of an Edgar Allan Poe type. Poe was terrified of being buried alive. This poor old man was scared of being burnt to death.

Damien's mother answered the door. Trass's eyes got bigger and bigger as she heard the rattling of keys and the bolts being pulled back from the huge metal door. Then, this tiny woman, with car keys in one hand and a big fat baby under her arm, pulled the door open wide.

'I can't shake hands. I'm Jo Kelleher. Damien said you were coming over. He's in the house somewhere. Either yell up the stairs or get one of the others to hunt him out.'

Trass looked at me and I looked at her. We both smiled at Mrs Kelleher. In the hallway were three bikes, a big old fashioned pram and a headless doll which a small wispy-blonde child of about three snatched up and ran off with.

'That's Cassie. She's the reason for nuts and bolts,' Mrs Kelleher explained. 'She broke out of her cot at nine months, her play-pen a week later and has been getting to be more like Houdini every day. Anyway, I must dash. I have to pick up Marc, the father figure. Go straight down.' She pointed along the hall to another metal door in the distance. 'I've left a batch of buns on the table in the kitchen. Grab them quickly. Otherwise the rest of the horde will have them. See you in a while.' And with that she was gone.

Trass and I looked at each other again. Without saying a word we agreed: Damien and his family were very definitely different! And we both liked his mum.

Twenty-nine

We stood for a second watching Cassie. She was attempting to climb into a battered pedal car, organise her doll to one side and her shopping basket to the other.

'Do you know where Damien is?' I asked.

I'm not used to small kids. Ben, the cousin, is horribly spoilt. I once pushed him off the swing in his garden by mistake (I think it was by mistake); he yelled for hours. That was my first impression of a screaming brat.

'You talk funny,' replied Cassie.

Trass really laughed at that.

'I don't.'

'You do.'

Damien came leaping down the stairs. I'd never seen him in anything but the awful grey uniform. Now, in faded jeans, a sweater designed for an elephant and bare feet, he looked ... he looked, brilliant.

'Cassie will keep you at that for hours. Mum reckons she's a leftover from the Spanish Inquisition. Cassandra Kelleher, be gone! Scoot!'

She didn't say anything; she looked very hard at Damien and then at us. For a split second I could have sworn I saw her stick up a solitary finger in defiance. But that's not possible. Or is it? I have a feeling that anything might be possible with the Kellehers.

Damien's room is on the second floor. It's full of computer equipment, old televisions which he repairs and resells, and masses of electronic gear. He's definitely following in his father's footsteps. Trass was so quiet at first that I was afraid it had been a bad idea to rush her into meeting more people. But then she met up with Toby - he's the next brother down. Toby goes to a different school because he's keen on sports. He and Trass disappeared to somewhere else in the house. Toby isn't only a rugby fanatic: he also plays keyboard and acoustic guitar.

The house is fantastic. It has wide hallways and there is this constant banging as one metal door is closed and another opened. Faces without names kept appearing. Damien did try to tell me. There's Cassie and her twin Chris. Obviously there's Damien and Toby. The baby is called Tomas, not Thomas. Somewhere in between is Ophelia, Sophie, Darragh and Hugh. What a collection!

It was while Damien was showing me an ancient photograph of the man who designed and built the place, that Enda appeared. Anyone who can look good in school uniform can't fail to look great in home clothes. She looked stunning. I'd like to like her because Damien seems to, but when she saw Damien and me alone, she gave me one of her punching stares. She must have practised it for hours. It is quite something, midway between a snarl and a smile.

As Trass and I were walking back to my house, I asked her how she would feel about living in a house.

'It'd be odd at first but it's something I keep thinking about. Mum would hate it, I'm sure. But I'm different. Every time I start at a school, I wonder what it would be like to get to know people for a long time.'

Suddenly I felt guilty about being so selfish. My life's pretty simple by comparison with Trass's. She seems to get on with it. What's more, when I asked how she coped with her mother, she seemed surprised.

'How do you mean?' she asked.

'Well, don't you tell her that you don't want to move? Don't you argue with her that it doesn't suit you? That it doesn't help when it comes to making friends?'

'No. I don't always agree with her, but she's my mother and loyalty is something terribly important to travellers. With so many outsiders against us, we have to stick together, take care of one another.'

I like that. And I suspect that I've been overdosing on disloyalty quite a lot recently. Obviously I'm going to have to make a bigger effort if I want Trass to stay being my friend.

By the time we got back to the house it was already eight o'clock. I had to ask mum to give Trass a lift home. She's pretty good about that. In fact she's not bad about a lot of things, when I'm thinking straight. Help! I don't want to like my dramatic, self-absorbed mother. But I suppose I do. Sometimes.

When we returned, I decided the time had come to discuss what's been on my mind for a while. Time my revelation came to the surface and we really try to help Trass. We were just pulling into the garage when I opened my mouth to begin. Then, suddenly, out dashes Ed, looking remarkably well for a runaway. Mum leapt out of the car. I darted round the other side and Ed bear-hugged the pair of us. Peter Graylocks stood on the top step of the house, beaming down like a fond uncle. If only he weren't such a creep!

Even Puss joined in the fun by climbing into the car and squatting elegantly with what looked like a smile on his face, and then proceeded to pee everywhere. Mother didn't seem to care. She will tomorrow. I'd better get up early and see what disinfectant does to car seats. I don't suppose I can shove them in the bin if it doesn't work out!

Thirty

Thank Heavens it's the weekend. Sleep deprivation makes you go mad. I think I'm a likely candidate. We sat up until after two, talking, drinking coffee, laughing, explaining to Ed what things are like here. Suddenly I found all sorts of positive stuff to say. In fact, mum and I must have sounded like representatives from the Irish Tourist Board. Ed says he's never going to leave. Luckily Peter had to go home early; he had surgery in the morning. I hope Puss gave his car the same treatment as ours!

I was right. Ed hitched to Fishguard, in Wales, caught a boat and landed in Rosslare. When I told him he could have got a boat which would have brought him into Cork, he almost throttled me. Imagine, we've both learned to hitch in the last few days. Mum was very serious about that. She has threatened a cutting off of funds for the two of us if we try it again. No matter how often I told her that everyone does it here, she would not be convinced.

I don't care, Ed is here and he's safe and he's staying. He says he wants to get a job and forget school. Fat chance of that happening. If I know our mother she'll have him booked into a school so fast he won't even notice how itchy the uniform is, until it's too late!'

I'd love mum to meet Mrs Kelleher; she's so warm. Being in their house yesterday was so different from here. She was doing homework with one of the smaller ones, feeding the baby, rescuing Cassie from the top of the fridge freezer. In amongst all the noise and activity she was calm and interested. She wanted to know all about Trass, about England, how it feels to be here. No wonder Damien is like he is: he's allowed to live his own life. I wish mum could be like that, stable.

I must tell mum about Toby's school. Ed likes rugby too. Ed was supportive about the animal thing and vegetarianism. He said that getting to know about the world and what we can and cannot do to it makes sense.

'Do you know something, Ness - it's going to be up to our generation to undo all the harm of the last century. They call it progress, I think it's more pro mess. But we're going to have to try.'

It's so good having Ed back.

In all the excitement I almost forgot when I woke up that Aideen was coming over. I'd waited so long, I couldn't believe that today had arrived. Whilst busily studying myself in the bedroom mirror, and finding to my horror that spots have now crept from my face on to my back, the doorbell rang. Charging down the stairs in my pyjamas, the top of which prove the point that I need a size larger, I opened the door. Clara caught my eye first, but that was not surprising. She had arrived back from Dublin and stuck on her cheek was a massive plaster with *rabid* in sunshine yellow written across it. I wonder what her mother thinks of that?

Behind her was Sorcha with Aideen. It had to be Aideen. Hers was the only face I didn't recognise. They all knew each other. Apparently Aideen and Clara went to play-school in Bishopstown together, then Clara's dad had moved them here and they'd lost touch. That's something else that I find odd about Cork: everyone seems to know everyone else. They're related or know a friend who knows you. I asked Sorcha about it.

'This is a very little island when you think about it, Ness. If we travel away from it, we have to get back, even if it's for a short while. I have an aunt who lives in the States but although she's been there for more than twenty years she still refers to Ireland as home. We are all connected. It makes us feel secure. Occasionally it's a nuisance. If you make a mistake everyone seems to have heard about it! But on the whole it works.'

She could only stay for a little while but made a big point of asking me how things are going and promised that she hadn't forgotten me.

I showed Clara and Aideen up to my little bedroom and darted into the bathroom to get dressed. It was lucky I did, because even though it was only ten in the morning the doorbell rang again. This time it was Damien, Enda and Toby. In amongst all the feet and chucked down coats, Ed walked into my room, not realising how full it was. Looking at me oddly he said, 'I thought you didn't know anyone.'

Enda positively fell over herself to be introduced to my brother (she isn't the kind of girl who would actually fall over: that's more my style). Damien winked at me. I'm not sure what he meant by it. Within seconds Trass appeared.

In England mum would have had a fit. All those

99

people, with music blaring from my stereo. Clara and Aideen were lying on the bed with their shoes on. Ed, semi-dressed, as usual, was looking for a clean T-shirt. Mum didn't say a word, just mentioned that she was off out to do the shopping and was there anything that Ed needed.

'Mrs Dineen is in the kitchen baking enough scones to feed an army. Go on down when you're all ready. I'll be back in a while.'

I could see Damien looking approvingly at my mother. She's still in jeans. I hope she's over the suit and high heels phase. That's ok when you're trying to impress. But I don't think my mum is that sort. Deep down she's a muddle head. That's what dad used to call her.

She looks impressive anyway.

Thirty-one

'Are my jeans around, Mrs Dineen?' Everything is sparkling in the kitchen. Even Puss's water dish has been lovingly polished. Thanks, Mrs D.

Mum gave up on our old house in England; that's why Posie hated it so much. It was always chaotic. I bet the headmaster's wife keeps a neat home. I can almost see her ironing his shirts, in between rowing with their daughter. I think when mum had the first, little place, she understood where everything was. What was expected of her. But once dad started knocking things down, putting things up, she lost direction. That's probably why she chose this one; it's an in between size. It's odd the way I saw it at first, big, forbidding. I was so angry.

'In the hot press, pet.' Hot press, there's another funny set of words. Airing cupboard. If I keep saying it to myself, then I won't forget the old name. 'Oh Puss!' He's lying on top of the towels, stretched fully out, purring contentedly and pretending to be a handsome Bengal overlord. In amongst the warmth of the dried clothes he is master of all! 'You will be in trouble, my friend, if a certain person, who will remain nameless, finds you.' Picking him up I grab my jeans. What to wear is the problem. Seeing as I look lumpy in everything, I opt for the biggest, baggiest jumper I can find. It's an old one of dad's. Mum gave most of his stuff away. It was horrible. This man arrived in a van and simply collected the suitcases she had filled. He didn't say anything except thank you. I wonder who's walking around in dad's suits, wearing his shoes? He'd have approved though, he liked the idea of recycling. Anyway, Ed and I took his jerseys, some of his shirts and T-shirts. When I feel miserable, wearing something that he once wore helps, a bit.

'Did you find the jeans, Ness?' Mrs Dineen calls up the stairs. Leaving Puss nestling on my discarded school skirt I pray that he remembers the pact that we have made with each other - he can share my bed as long as he heads for the hills when it's toilet time.

'I was making some batter and I thought I'd pop some of these mushrooms in the remainder of it. Here, have a taste.' Mrs Dineen is a genius. 'Well?' she asks. Her face is shiny because she's been working in the hot kitchen. She's old enough to be my grandmother, but she couldn't be more different. Mum's parents are dead but dad's are still alive. Stupid, isn't it? Grandad has arthritis and Grandma never stops criticizing. It doesn't make sense that they're still around.

Mrs Dineen is always busy, not bossy - get - out - of - my - way busy. She does interesting things. 'They're delicious,' I say. She smiles with pleasure. 'Would you like to learn a few recipes?' She asks. 'I'd love to, as long as it isn't today. I'm going over to a friend's house.' Now I feel guilty. 'Today, tomorrow, you let me know. Now, where's Master Puss. It's time I put him in the garden.'

Isn't she special! No guilt, no long face. She has six children, well, not children, three boys and three girls, grown up; none of them live here. She has grandchildren in England, Australia and America. One of her sons is a priest in Peru. She's very proud of him. But the important thing is, that even though she must

102

get lonely at times, she's moved with the times. Like the cat thing, to mum he's so much trouble, to Mrs Dineen he's part of the family.

'Does your brother like Charlotte?' she asks, having stroked a very annoyed looking Puss before closing the door on him. 'I don't know what it is,' I say. Charlotte? Bronte, Rampling, Corday?

'It's a pudding, made with apples. We've some beautiful apples. I'll have it ready for him. I've cooked a ham. That will be tasty cold. And, good health or whatever, there's a pound of good Irish butter in the fridge. You can't be eating that watery margarine after a journey.'

Isn't that amazing. All my doom and gloom, dispelled. If I knew how, and if I knew her well enough, I'd talk to her. But I don't.

Thirty-two

'So, what are we going to do?' Ed, half way through his sixth scone, with crumbs on his chin and a smile on his face, asked the whole lot of us, Mrs Dineen included, sitting round the table. I wonder if Mrs Dineen dreams anymore. What do old people dream about?

'Shop,' Enda offered. No takers for that.

'Go to Fota,' Clara's idea.

'Too far, too expensive, too cold. What about bowling?' Aideen suggested.

'What's Fota?' It sounded interesting but quite what a Fota is I didn't know.

'You wait, we'll go there in the spring, take a picnic. It's a huge wild life park. You'll love it, Ness. It's your kind of place. Ostrich eggs scattered around the grass like snooker balls. Ring tailed lemurs who hop on to your shoulder and eat anything they can lay their sticky little hands on - we'll bring apples and peanuts. And there are some black and white monkey type creatures who appear from nowhere. They slowly sidle down trees and grab fruit. Won't she love it, Aideen?' Clara obviously likes Fota.

'Yes, but not today. That'll take a bit of planning and a lot of saving, between the train and the charge to get in.'

'Maybe mum will drive us over some time. I'd love to see it. Are there lions and elephants?' It all sounded too good to be true, a place where I could touch the creatures. Being sensible, I suppose the idea of having lions wandering around wasn't too bright. I'd been to Windsor Safari park and frankly I was disappointed. The best bit was the wolves. They looked like great dogs padding, listening, running. It's a real pity people are so prejudiced against them.

'So, how about it, bowling and then back here to listen to music and find out what Vanessa thinks of us all? What about you, Ed? Where are you going to go to school? What about the Leaving? Do you think you'll be able to pick up on that?'

Aideen has black hair, shaved underneath and long on top, her eyes dance and her voice has a catch in it, like a laugh. I love the accent. She's another personality, like Clara. She's instant. I could have known her for weeks, years even, yet it's only hours.

'School, that is up to our venerable mother,' Ed replied with a shudder. I know how he feels.

'I suspect I might need an extra year. Ness reckons that your school, Toby, sounds the right place for me. Don't tell me it's the Christian Brothers! I'm sure Uncle Tony is a closet Jesuit, waiting to mould me in his image.'

Uncle Tony and Ed do not get on any more. Apparently he disapproved of Charlie, Ed's ex-girlfriend, because she dressed totally in black. He loathed Ed's friends: he called them recidivists, whatever that is. As for his music, it seems our uncle is not into Gothic! The final insult was when Ed refused to baby-sit instantly, without warning, whether or not he had other plans. Can you blame him for being slightly anti-uncle at the moment?

Toby doesn't look anything like Damien. He's taller for a start, with very short hair. He's more reserved, thoughtful, less extravagant with his hands. Damien's are forever moving to explain something in amongst the torrent of what he has to say. Trass and Toby really seem to like one another. Every so often Enda looks across at them. All they're doing is talking, quietly. What is she thinking about as she watches them?

'Why don't we all meet up tomorrow?' Toby suggested. 'Ma feels unwanted if the house isn't crammed with extra bodies and the kettle permanently on the boil. You'll come, won't you, Trass?' Toby's idea of us all going over is exactly what I would have planned, if I could have planned anything. Trass agreed and Ed thought it sounded like a good idea. Only Enda looked less than convinced.

At this point we were all brought to order by Mrs Dineen. 'Right. I have a bit of clearing up to do. Off you go, bowling, shopping, whatever. This old cat needs a spot of peace and I've an apple tart and bread to make.'

We started to clear away plates and mugs but Mrs Dineen insisted that she would be far happier doing it herself. As we trooped down the drive I could hear Toby saying to Ed, 'Seriously, my dad used to go to St Pats. They sent Damien to the City School because of the computer technology department. They reckon they're going to have to send Cassie straight to a correction centre. The word bold doesn't begin to cover what she gets up to.'

Funny, it's back to language again. Bold means brave to me. Here it means very naughty. It'll be good having Ed around to learn the differences. I hope mum realises how stupid it was to split us up in the first place.

It's Saturday, it's raining and we're all going bowling.

Thirty-three

Damien quizzed Ed all the way into the Mardyke - that's where the bowling alley is - about Colchester, computer shops, computer courses.

Sometimes Cork looks so sad. Old hamburger containers lie scattered in the gutter, broken cider bottles and cans are pushed behind railings near the court house. The uncleared rubbish reminds me that some people were out the night before, walking the streets, fighting and sleeping rough. I'd never seen a beggar until I crossed the bridge to the big new shopping centre here. She was a bit older than me, with a baby in a scruffy pushchair. The baby wasn't hers. The girl was too young, but her face was as pale as Trass's. And the cup she had to beg with was an old drinking cup, plastic, faded pink, the sort smallies use with a lid on. The lid was off and there was maybe thirty pence at the bottom. I couldn't look at her, not into her eyes. I certainly couldn't put a few pennies in that container. It would be an insult. She probably thought I thought I was better than her because I didn't give her anything. That wasn't it at all. But what I do know is that I have to do something for Trass even if I can't help that girl. The problem is, how can I help either of them?

The bowling was great. Toby is very good. Clara's crazy attempts had us all aching with laughter. Enda half-heartedly ran up with the ball in her hand and consistently missed.

'I don't know how you do it. It's so difficult,' she said to any male within hearing distance.

Irritated, and to prove that it wasn't that hard, I managed to score a strike twice. Venom rather than skill drove me on.

'Not bad,' Aideen shouted to me after I cleared the deck. 'Have you tried camogie yet? I can see you with a hurley and a sliotar, crowned with a helmet - you might even keep your brain in place! I bet there's a team at your school. You ought to give it a whirl.'

Aideen's humour is so lively! She bubbles and bounces and never stops talking. I wonder if she worries about anything?

'Camogie. What's that?' Between Fota, a sliotar and camogie I'm into a brand new world of words!

'It's like hurling,' she began. I looked confused. Hurling. I'd never heard of that either.

'Think of a mad man's version of hockey,' Ed interrupted, while waving his arms about with a pretend stick in his hands.

'You'll love it. You get to chase and run and belt at a ball. Give it a try. But ... '

And with that Aideen rolled up the leg of her jeans. There on display was the biggest bruise I've ever seen, wonderful yellows and blues.

'I did that on Monday. Take it as a reminder. Wear shin pads. You keep your teeth with the guard on your helmet and you hang on to your legs with the pads.' I was useless at hockey. Dare I try something even more dangerous?

Enda visibly shook at the thought of camogie. Pushing towards Ed she confided that the only game she played was tennis, doubles, mixed.

'You'd look good in white,' he said. If Ed gets involved with her I will kill him. He cannot be serious.

'Tell me about Enda,' Ed asked, lying on my bed, hands behind his head.

The others have all gone but Aideen is staying the night. I can hear her splashing around in the bathroom, listening to music and singing along to it.

'What about her? She's fourteen' (too young for you), 'has been going out with Damien for a year' (I think. I don't really know). 'Looks good' (that's all too obvious) 'and ... '

'You don't like her.' Ed can read me like a book.

'It's not so much that I don't like her, more that I'm not like her.'

'Ness, you've got some great mates here. The whole lot of you talk, get on, know how to make each other laugh. I like that. Enda is a bit different from the rest of you. But someone like Damien wouldn't be going around with her unless she's worth it.'

I'd thought the same thing. Damien seems straightforward, no nonsense, yet he puts up with Enda fawning over Ed and Toby. It's revolting. She's always acting.

'I'll give it a bit more effort.' I'm not convinced but there's no harm in trying.

What is it about certain people, no matter how hard I try I cannot like them? Dad would have said something sensible like, it takes all sorts to make the world. With Aideen and Ed I feel happy. Trass and I got on immediately: we were pulled together by feeling lonely. I suppose I admire Clara and she makes me laugh. But Enda is trying to prove something all the time. I know she's attractive, I'm not envious of that. But if I talk to Damien or Toby and she notices, it's as if I'm walking on holy ground. And now she wants to get her claws into Ed. I can feel it.

I don't want Damien as a boyfriend. I want him as a boy friend. She wouldn't be able to see the difference. I'm not stupid. There is something between Damien and me but I'm not prepared to lose that something for a practice kiss and a cuddle that could wreck everything. I want to get to know him and his family. Yet fancying someone, sex I suppose, does get in the way. I refuse to be tongue-tied around boys I like. It doesn't happen with the girls I know. I want to learn how to relax and be me when I'm with Damien. That isn't impossible, is it?

I hope Ed isn't attracted to Enda. That would be the end! It's like a wire pulling at you, this meeting with boys you like. I want all sorts of people in my life, girls, boys, old, young, that doesn't matter; what matters is that we click. I'll have to see what tomorrow is like, over at the Kellehers.

Thirty-four

Disaster. I think I've managed to alienate Trass, Aideen, my mother, my brother, the whole Kelleher clan, and Enda. Enda I can cope with.

Everything was going beautifully. We went to Church, had a big Sunday dinner. Mum cooked vegetable lasagne for me and a roast for Aideen, Ed and herself. Puss was thrilled. He snarled over the fatty bits like a demented tiger. Some creatures are naturally blood thirsty. Then we went to Damien's.

Mum was fascinated by all the nuts and bolts at the front door. Cassie and her twin Chris were dressed in their Sunday best. They looked like an advertisement for perfect children, that is until Chris ran off with Cassie's headless doll. Instantly Cassie tore after her brother, having let out a four letter yell. Once she caught him she threw him on the ground and beat him up, then retrieved her precious, decapitated friend, returned to my mother, climbed on her knee, placed a free thumb in her mouth and looked the picture of innocence. Mrs Kelleher just laughed, picked up the howling Chris and carried on pouring tea and serving sandwiches.

Marc, the dad, was talking to Ed about Saint Patrick's, the school Toby goes to. It sounds great. Everything was going exactly as I wished until I heard Mrs Kelleher mention some houses the council have recently acquired with a view to letting them to any travellers who might be ready to settle.

'There are a few Councillors who see the need to provide serviced halting sites, plus as I said these houses. They're quite near here; in fact, one or two local residents are already up in arms about the idea.'

Trass was totally silent. I don't even know if she heard the whole conversation. There was a fair amount of noise in the kitchen.

'I'm not surprised. No offence, Trass, but where do you put those sort of drop-outs?' Enda's eyes roved around. Skipping past me she fixed Trass with a smile.

All afternoon Enda had been fussing over Ed and he seemed to like it. Mr Kelleher went out of his way to clear a space at the table for her, find her an uncracked cup. I could feel myself getting more and more annoyed. I looked over at Damien. He was half listening to us, half watching some match on the television. Without thinking, I dived in.

'Wouldn't it be great, Trass? Do you think your mother and grandfather might consider staying?'

It was what I'd been thinking about, my revelation. I knew that Trass's mum was unhappy about moving yet again. The grandfather is very old. They both love Trass. Maybe this was just the solution, a prayer answered.

'Ness, being English you couldn't possibly understand the problem,' Enda interrupted. 'You wouldn't want to move into somewhere permanent, would you?' tossing her head and waiting for a reply she stared at Trass, challenging her.

Damien looked up. Mr and Mrs Kelleher, the twins, the baby, Toby, the whole room, which seconds ago had been a seething, warm, human place, became silent, focussed on one person, Trass. Even Aideen, the unstoppable talker who'd been noisily playing snap with three excitable small Kellehers, went quiet.

I'd seen Trass upset twice before. Once on that first day at school when she felt ill and alone. Then at the hospital when she was worried about Clara. I knew she was capable of getting angry. I'd seen it in my bedroom. But I had no idea how coldly angry she could be.

'I've known Ness for a week, no, less than that. In the little time we've been together she has never watched me in her house, just in case I pocket the silver or run off with her radio.'

Mum stopped drinking tea. She was blushing slightly. Maybe she had considered that possibility.

'Right now I look like you, Enda,' Trass continued. 'We're wearing the same uniform for once.'

Yes, I had to agree with that. Jeans and such are the home uniform, I suppose. Then I understood what she was getting at. She was forced to look different because at school she doesn't wear the horrible grey uniform. Long live individuality, if only it didn't hurt so much.

'I want to stop moving. Ness appreciates why. Starting again and again hurts. It's called loneliness, Enda.'

Mum suddenly looked very tired and very sad. Old. Ed got up and went over to her, protectively. I like that. Ed isn't all hugs and kisses and lovey stuff but he is around when you need him.

Enda sat, looking bored, very decoratively bored but, nonetheless, unimpressed. Damien and the rest continued to listen.

'Ness hates being in Ireland a lot of the time. She

113

would love things to be like they were. Both of us know that's not possible. It can't happen. I think I would have liked a traveller for a father. Then at least my mother wouldn't be living in a cold caravan trailing after my grandfather who is getting too old to do the work he's used to, and too proud because of our traditions to ask for help.'

Enda let out a hiss of sorts and said under her breath, but so that everyone could hear, 'work!'

'What Ness has are manners. I like that. She says things straight out and I'm going to do the same. You don't like me for what I am and I don't like you for what you are. That makes me no better than you. But at least what goes on inside me isn't only what you see on the outside.'

Now Enda was angry. I felt embarrassed. What would Damien think of me, of Trass? Two mopers who couldn't cope, perhaps?

'You've heard the saying,' Enda began, fiddling with the tiny gold watch on her wrist, 'you can't make a leopard change its spots. Well, that, I'm afraid, is the situation we have with you knackers.'

It was when she said knackers, making it sound like something dirty, reminding me of my humiliation at Patrice's hands, that I snapped. I jumped up and shouted, 'You stuck up, overdressed, fawning ... ' and then I was stuck for a word. I was not going to cry, or stop. Now I'd begun I needed them all to know what I thought of her. My mother was in a state of shock. Sorry, mum. Ed looked stunned. Whether it was Enda or me who'd produced that effect didn't matter right then. Damien had picked up Cassie who was crying. I shouldn't have shouted. Then it came to me. I looked at

114

Enda with the long hair, soft mouth, slim wrists, everything just so, except her frightening attitude towards people. Apologies, lady dogs.

'Bitch!'

I ran out of the kitchen, up the long hallway, threw open the huge metal front door which someone had mercifully forgotten to bolt, and ran home. How could they listen to her? Why didn't they stop her? Why does everything constantly have to shift.

And why can't I keep my large mouth tightly shut?

Thirty-five

It's three in the morning, nearly Monday and school. Ed has just gone to his room.

'You were right, Ness. She's not like you.'

Enda. No, she's not like me.

Aideen, Trass, Damien, Toby and Ed came back for me. God knows what I looked like. I was crying because I was angry, ashamed, hurt. Damien tried to explain that Enda's background is complicated; her mother and father are successful business people who are rarely at home.

'That's no excuse. Why don't you get angry with her?' I asked, hiccuping through my drippy nose. Crying is not a glamorous activity. Neither is sniping at someone's girlfriend.

'I don't think any of us would put up with her if we weren't related. That includes mum, but because she's her niece she keeps on working at it,' Toby exploded.

'Your cousin! I thought she was your girlfriend, Damien,' I let out with a gasp, followed by a blushing session which made my ears burn. At this stage I must have looked like a clown in full makeup.

'Girlfriend! Give me credit,' laughed Damien. 'I felt sorry for her. When she started at school, she was so stiff and starchy no one could stand her. She was used to some posh, private place in Dublin. Then when her dad became European Sales and Marketing President, or whatever the grand title is he's forever shoving down mum's throat ... I think he thinks his little sister has done very badly for herself. Anyway, they moved near us so that Enda could stay when they go off on one of their jaunts abroad.'

It was coming clear, Enda's need for protectiveness; she must see Toby and Damien as brothers. Mr Kelleher being so nice, he's trying to make her feel wanted, special. And now Ed has seen through the sham. I suppose she must feel abandoned in some ways, what with her parents jetting around. I like Toby and Damien's loyalty, not only to Enda but to me as well. Most importantly, I have to remember not to bottle things up; if I have a question, then I should ask it. Not asking anything about Enda for this long was a big mistake, as my explosion proved. I've upset quite a few friends today.

Trass told me that she is going to talk seriously to her mother about staying for a while longer. But she feels guilty that she's going to try and make her mother change, just for her. Apparently, after I left so unceremoniously, Trass informed Enda that she intends to go right through school and maybe college, then perhaps she could help the travelling community and educate others about such things as knackers, tinkers, gypsies and travellers. Enda, furious, had called Trass and 'her kind' a bunch of users.

'It's going to take a lot more than your half-hearted efforts at public relations to change the sensible minds of the majority,' Enda replied, sneering.

'I think it will be worth the effort, Trass,' mum had said at that point. 'You're on the right track.'

Ed said that mum was brilliant. When she came back, much later, she gave me a huge hug and told me she'd been wrong about Trass and that she had thoroughly enjoyed the Kellehers.

'I'm very proud of you, Ness. Although,' and she said this with a grin, 'bitch was not only inaccurate but also a little hard.'

Aideen asked if she could come back next weekend.

'Life's more exciting around you lot. Screaming matches over cups of afternoon tea, planned visits to County Hall to wave banners at Councillors and a beheaded rat at the front door when we got back. What more can a bored teenager ask for?'

My head hurts. Crying does that to me. And I've forgotten to iron my school shirt; it's in the washing basket downstairs. I can hear rain against the window. I haven't even thought about my project. Right now I'm a hungry vegetarian.

Mum told me she's going to visit Trass's mum with Mrs Kelleher. They are three very different women. I wonder what the outcome will be? Apparently Mrs K has a Councillor friend who has been pushing for improved conditions for knackers, as Enda calls them. What a revolting word. Mum tried to explain some of the settled community's fear to me, how there's an historical, even hysterical fear of anyone who looks or acts differently. Now that she's got to know Trass she's really determined to help.

Full of surprises, my mother. Nice one, dad! Maybe she's not such a tyrant, well, not all the time.

Thirty-six

Ed's breakfasts are incredible. They are a heart specialist's nightmare, cholesterol gone crazy; everything is fried; even the tea tastes greasy.

My school shirt smells like a chip shop. I just hope spraying it with deodorant will cover some of the aroma. Ironing it in amongst the fried bread, eggs, bacon, sausages, pudding, mushrooms and tomatoes added a lot of life to the morning. Poor Mrs Dineen. Will she ever recover from the combined terror of my brother and my cat?

Handing rinds from the rashers to the meat monster, Ed offered me fresh juice, having carefully snipped off the top of the carton. He's learning, thanks to Mrs Dineen. She leaves scissors, on a string, on a hook, by the kettle.

'I have an appointment at Saint Patrick's at nine with the head. Mum seems to think it's just a matter of going along and smiling sweetly. What do you think, Ness? Will I be able to absorb five extra subjects?'

Ed was doing sciences in England but is now going to have to take on some others. He's a worker; he'll be all right. I've put one week behind me in a new school. He's got to go through all that. Poor thing.

'It's lucky I'll recognise one friendly face,' he said, spooning sugar into his tea and spreading marmalade on the fried bread. 'Toby's a good kid. He tells me they'll be doing rugby trials for the first team next weekend. I can't wait.'

Ed's totally back to normal. For a while, after dad died, he went a bit off the rails. Mum caught him drinking vodka and smoking cigarettes. She threw a huge tantrum (which didn't help) and threatened to have him taken into care. They bawled and yelled at one another. It's been a rough year. And I have a rough few hours ahead of me. I have to face Patrice, never mind seeing Enda again.

Walking into the classroom having given St Michael, still looking pleased with himself, another hard stare, I sat down and waited. It wasn't early, well after eight fifty five; mum had given me a lift because we were running late. Where was everyone? I could feel myself beginning to panic. Maybe everyone had decided to gang up against me because of what I'd said to Enda. No, Damien told me that everything was 'cool'. Looking around the classroom I spotted the message on the blackboard. 'Mass for first, second and third years at nine o'clock. Holy Trinity Church.'

A note had been handed round on Friday, still at the bottom of my bag, still unread. It's all stupid Andrew's, let's-eat-a-pig-followed-by-a-lamb-or-two-for-elevenses fault. He and that discussion on vegetarianism made me forget everything. Why didn't one of the others say anything? I suppose the weekend was a bit eventful. Holy Trinity is just near our house. Great! The luxury of my lift to school was a total waste of time.

Grabbing my bag I ran all the way, past our house which looked peaceful, with smoke curling from the chimney. Clara's garden was full of leaves, and there was ivy I'd never seen before, red and green, climbing up one wall. Autumn is here.

I dashed up the white stone steps of the Church, at six minutes past nine and pushed open the ancient door into the dimly lit Church. The priest was already on the altar. I couldn't see one familiar face. So, with my head down, pressed against my chest, I began to walk down the aisle. Not again! Only me, alone! Where could I find a seat? Mortification. To think I was feeling sorry for Ed. One week on, things are just as terrible.

A hand pulled me into a pew. Damien pushed Catherine along to make room for me. She smiled. Damien gave me the famous wink. It's like a welcome mat, that gesture. Thank you. Clara, with a new plaster on her cheek, grinned at me. Trass looked happy. Even the droning from the altar about the moral responsibility of youth couldn't deflate me.

We are responsible. We don't understand certain things but on the whole we're open eyed and listening, learning. Don't talk down to us.

Thirty-seven

'Let's call back to my house and collect some tapes,' Clara suggested as we began to walk home after school. The rain was getting into everything, my feet were squelching and my hair had plastered itself against my head.

'You ought to cut it short. It suits you around your face like that,' Aideen, with her coat collar up, shouted above the roar of the traffic and the wind and the water. Damien was just walking past, jumping into puddles and laughing every time Enda squealed pathetically. 'She's right. It looks ok,' he called back. Isn't life unbelievable! There I was, soaking wet, drowning, while Miss - Barbie - goes - to - Hollywood, Enda, looked perfect. She had a wide-brimmed mobster felt hat, rakishly pulled over one eye. What is more, she glared at me angrily before linking arms between herself, Ed and Damien. My own brother, fooled, duped.

Clara's house smells of flowers, dried flowers and petals. All the rooms have little cut glass bowls of pot pourri, which her mum prepares. Wrinkling his nose, Damien whispered dramatically, 'It's either a brewery or the local opium den!' Clara chuckled as she tossed tapes into her bag.

'It keeps her occupied, saves her pulling the wings off nightingales. She tortures daisies instead.'

Clara seems so unlike her mother. It's not the size

thing, it's the whole thing. Mrs Farrell is precise, fussy. As we all walked in she told us, not asked us, to remove our shoes and coats. That's fine, not splooshing dirty rainwater and mud over her polished wood floor makes sense, but it would have made all the difference if she'd smiled, as she commanded. Some adults have the ability to ask you to do things without making you feel angry. Mrs Kelleher, for instance.

Yesterday taught me something, that's why I was conscious of Mrs Farrell's attitude. So much difference is made by the tone of your voice. I know that I use a harder sound for mum than I do for Mrs Dineen. The way Mrs Kelleher organizes everything is good humoured. She can get angry. It's not that she's a saint or anything. I do not think we would get on if she were. She was really annoyed with Damien and Toby who had rolled up newspapers and were sword fighting in the middle of the kitchen when one of the littler Kellehers got pushed over and started to whinge. 'Out, now,' she shouted. And they did, taking their rolls of newspaper with them to carry on swashbuckling in the hall.

But that was it. She didn't go on and on about it. She washed Cassie's hands and picked up Darragh, now crying miserably. 'You're a bit put out since Tomas arrived, aren't you, sweet?' Darragh, smug now that he was being noticed, stopped crying and helped himself to some currants which someone had picked out of the buns and left on the table.

'Right, I've got everything I need to educate you two space invaders about real Irish rock music,' Clara pronounced, nodding her head towards Ed and me. 'Now you are in the centre of the music business, you will have to get used to the best!' We followed her out.

I checked that the cushions were straight on the chairs. Mrs Farrell makes me jumpy. Calling to no one in particular, Clara said, 'Back in a decade or two.' We began to put on our wet clothes. Bustling into the hallway, Mrs Farrell checked the floor, again, and insisted that Clara put on a dry coat.

'I have, mum,' Clara sighed resignedly.

What age does her mother think she is? She's not a baby. When will parents grow up! Maybe I'm being hard, what with Clara's history of illness. But sometimes, if they don't say anything at all it works far better. Like the school skirt incident on Friday. I knew that I shouldn't have left the cat lying on it. Mrs Dineen knew that I should not have allowed him to dig his claws into it. What did she do? 'Ness, I've left the clothes brush and the sticky tape on your bed. When you've a moment, brush it clean and use the tape for the worst bits; that way, when you put it into the washing machine it will clean up nicely.'

Mrs Farrell, with all your airs and graces, Waterford glass bowls and wood block floors, I know someone who could teach you a lesson or two.

Thirty-eight

Enda is still very much part of the group but she isn't hanging on to Damien any more. Nothing has been said but the heavy duty ownership thing seems to have come to an end. She even offered to perm my hair the other day. I declined, as politely as possible. I have a sneaking suspicion she might end up making me look like Medusa. I can almost hear her apologising, then offering to shave my head to correct the mistake. That would be as good a way as any to get back at me. I might be wrong.

Everything in my life is going smoothly. Well, it was. Typical me, I had to go and change it. I decided to have a Hallowe'en party at our house. Parties are fun. This one might have been, had I not expansively invited the whole class. It's insane. Ed has promised to keep us all in order. Mum has been persuaded that it will be quite safe for her to leave us on our own. That was thanks to Mrs Dineen. I'm wandering around like a zombie. People like Patrice will be here, Andrew, some of the others I don't know all that well. What made me do it? I suspect I thought doing something stupendous would cement my being accepted. It's ridiculous; they liked me anyway.

Worrying about it is not going to get the sticks into the sausages. I hate touching meat. The cheese and pineapple was fine, but these pinky things are not pleasant. Trass has had a big chat with me about vegetarianism. She warned me that going on about it too much was getting boring. She also said that my not eating at the same time as mum and Ed was unfair on them. It made them feel awkward. She's a good mate, and she's absolutely right. I've even taken to doing some of my own cooking. It's not as good as Mrs Dineen's, not yet, but I'm coming on. Garlic mushrooms and baked potatoes with chives are my speciality. I'd better not eat garlic tonight. Bad breath as well as undisguised dread won't exactly make me the hostess of the year.

There are trays of crisps, peanuts in their shells, sandwiches of every shape and size. Clara helped me with those. She suddenly became creative and started cutting diamonds, stars and little men, with the pastry cutter. It all looks fine. I've splurged on loads of makeup. It's very pale. I thought seeing as I felt like a zombie I might as well look like one.

It's October the thirty-first and in exactly twenty minutes people will start to arrive. I feel sick. Uncle Tony and Aunt Fran plus Ben the creep and Wendy the winge are staying; just as was promised all that time ago in the graveyard. They appeared, almost hidden by bags of duty free, disposable nappies, and a remote control car, which is almost as big as the real thing, to keep Ben happy. Ed had a go with it and Ben screeched so loudly that any passer-by would have thought he was being murdered. Luckily the two poppets are staying with Mrs Dineen for the night!

I can hear Ed upstairs practising his drumming. He doesn't have drums here, so he's bashing away on empty biscuit tins. I wish he'd stop. He's happier now. Those first few weeks when he started school made him very sad. First of all it was the extra subjects. Then he didn't get into the first rugby team - he assumed it was a foregone conclusion that he would be on the list. But out of that came Toby's offer for him to join Toby's band. Aideen sings with them occasionally.

Mr Kelleher has an ancient drum kit. 'It looks like the one the Beatles used in "Help"', Ed remarked scathingly.

Anyway, after much scrubbing, polishing and buying new skins (they are not cheap but mother recognised that her son and heir required solid support at the time), he was ready to begin. Armed with hickory sticks (the best, according to Toby), Ed sat down and battered away.

The band meets on the top floor of the Kelleher's house. It's just as well, because those first few sessions were torture. After a week Ed was even getting some kind of rhythm out of them, and now, six weeks on, he's not bad at all.

Cassie always insists on sitting in on the practice sessions. With her thumb perpetually stuck in her mouth she taps away to the beat by pounding her doll up and down.

'You're sick, did you know that, Cass?' Toby told her.

She ignored him and went on beating time, well, more like beating the torso.

'Where's the head?' I once asked Mrs K.

'She flushed it down the loo: said she didn't like the face,' was her reply.

It's just as well for me that Cassie hasn't taken a dislike to my face.

I wish everyone would arrive. Listening for footsteps and cars above Ed's racket is hurting my ears. If I were in England I'd be getting ready for November the fifth, Guy Faulkes night. Poor old Guy, blowing up the Houses of Parliament probably seemed like a class idea all those hundreds of years ago. As he never made it across the sea to do the same to the Dáil (pronounced doorl. I'm getting quite good at Irish words), he doesn't even get a mention on the calendar. We used to have fun on Bonfire night. Dad would buy a big box of fireworks and mum would bake special food. The best treat of all was being allowed to hold a sparkler.

This is it. I can hear voices. Whatever made me think up this terrifying ordeal for myself? Pride, and you know what they say happens after it ... a great big fall!

Thirty-nine

Mum's last words as she left for some concert or other, were, 'Not too much mess, you two. We'll be back late, after one. Have the clearing up done.'

Then they departed, mum in a flurry of perfume and floaty scarves (she's into the nineteen twenties look at the moment), followed by Uncle Tony and Aunt Fran. I'm not sure what look Aunt Fran is into. She's very jumpy. I think she's petrified of Uncle Tony. I walked into the sitting room yesterday. She was lying on the sofa. But she leapt up when she heard me come in and said, 'I thought it was your uncle.'

Strange, aren't mothers/wives allowed to get tired?

Quite how mum imagined, with a lot of encouragement from me, that thirty-three extra people playing hallowe'en type games, wouldn't make a wreck of the place, is now beyond me. Apple bobbing for instance. It sounds innocent enough, but Clara managed to crack a back tooth on a fifty pence piece I had generously provided, well stuck into the smallest apple at the bottom of the bowl. The tooth hurt, but the bowl falling on to the floor, emptying its contents, just as someone was carrying through a tray of drinks, which inevitably joined the water and the tray carrier on the ground, could not have been predicted.

When you are a bit up tight, which I was, you seem to make silly suggestions. We were playing the flour mountain, you know, plate of flour, a cherry on the top and you have to nose in to find money hidden in the mountain. Was it worth it for twenty pence? No! My idea was that if the cherry got dislodged without finding anything you had to dip your face in water. Not even a remotely sensible suggestion.

Murder in the dark got a bit out of hand as well. It was very lucky that Wendy wasn't trying to get her beauty sleep. She would have yelled 'til Christmas at the noise made by wild teenagers careering up and down the stairs, flapping sheets and firing water pistols. The firing of water pistols came as a big surprise to Ed and me. Some creep sneaked in a plastic bag full of them. I spotted a couple of boys taking the bag outside, and warned them not to bring them in. A warning was not enough.

Most of them have gone. To think I was worried about the food. One or two, having grown weary of eating, picked up the remains and started to fling stuff round the room. I know half of them wouldn't dare even put their elbows on the table at home, but because they were here they did whatever they liked. If I weren't so angry I'd be upset. Ed did his best to keep things under control but he couldn't be in every room at the same time.

The mess is colourful, even picturesque - that's hysteria coming out. I am so very glad it's over. If only we had a fleet of cleaners waiting to help, we might just get away with it, with an added small miracle as a guarantee. Damien and Ed are upstairs trying to unblock the sink. Patrice had been drinking cider before she arrived and was violently ill after about ten minutes being here. She is so crass. She ruined her night, destroyed her mother's best button-through skirt she was wearing as a witch's cloak and lost a couple of her hangers-on, Dora and Caroline. They are really sound; right now they're in mum's bedroom (my old one; oh, how that carpet suffers!) trying to remove ground-in kohl. Why couldn't it have been something else? Kohl, you know it, black, squidgy and totally resistant to any known household carpet cleaner. I bet it was Andrew. He was wandering about with painted black lips, but then so were a pile of others. I didn't even recognise some of them.

Clara and Trass are in the kitchen with Aideen. Toby has just announced that the vacuum cleaner has seized up. I'm not surprised. Puss is now an Afro cat. He started to eat his way through the remains of the flour mountain. What is wrong with that animal? Anyway, because it was raining outside, and inside, I suppose, what with the water pistols, his amazing damp coat is now solidified with gluey flour. Yuk! Having padded around the work surfaces with sooty paws he has fallen asleep on the remains of the curled up sandwiches. I'll move him later. Quite how I'm going to clean him I haven't worked out. The house is the priority and we're running out of time.

Mum is due back at any minute. I am never having a party again. This isn't just too much mess. It's too much.

Forty

'Toast, Vanessa?' Mum to me. I'm back to being Vanessa since last night. It's ten thirty, the morning after the party and no, all our best efforts at clearing up were definitely not good enough in the cold light of day. There is something about pale November sunshine. It picks out the tiniest speck of dust, never mind glaring trails of spilt coke and apple cores chucked behind chairs. We didn't even notice them last night.

There I was, slumbering, exhausted, when mother barged into the room, tripping over Aideen, who didn't move. My covers were pulled back and I was told to be downstairs, now!

'Edward, stop what you are doing and sit.' Ed is half wearing a shirt. He looks baffled. He's still asleep. The body is there but the brain is resting. He's growing his hair and wants an earring. Mother is not impressed although it's not the shirt, hair and earring that are on her mind now. It's her kitchen table.

'I understand, Vanessa and Edward, that large numbers of young people gathered together in a house with insufficient parental supervision can go wild.'

Here we go. I deserve it. Ed doesn't. It was also a dig at Mrs Dineen. She dropped Ben and Wendy off a few minutes ago and promptly disappeared. Wise woman. If only I hadn't enlisted her help all this would probably never have happened. Mum had said then that no right-minded parent would leave a bunch of youngsters (I hate that word) on their own. She wasn't wrong. I'll say sorry to Mrs Dineen later.

Ben is watching Ed from the corner of the kitchen. He's found a squashed sausage roll and keeps offering it to Puss (still unwashed) and then pulling it away again. Wait for it, any second now.

'Aaahh ... mummmmyyyy.'

That's got rid of Ben. I knew the cat would finally live up to expectations. Maybe Ben will have to have a tetanus injection. It would be a very appropriate souvenir from Cork.

'Are you listening, Vanessa? Who did this?' I am listening.

Only a real trouble maker, someone malicious, would scratch letters on the table. Even if I didn't like it, I wouldn't do that to it.

'What does B.A.I.T. mean?' she asks, her voice quivering. How do I know what BAIT means. I didn't do it. None of my friends did it. I don't know anyone who would. Hold on. I get up and take a closer look.

'That's not BAIT. It's BRIT and there's one person I know who likes that word.'

Ed and I say it together, 'Patrice.'

I'd told Ed about my experience at the hands of Patrice. He was appalled and concerned. More than that, he was still angry with her. He'd wanted to talk to her last night but because of her rapid departure hadn't had the opportunity. Then it all came out.

Ed tries to explain to mum that Patrice had been drinking. Mum goes through her shock, horror routine. How could such a thing happen in her house et cetera. No matter how much we tell her that Patrice was the only one, she will not listen. Uncle Tony is trying to find antiseptic for Ben. Why did he have to arrive at this point?

'It's a disgrace. You'll have to ring the headmaster. The parents should be told. I cannot understand the lack of control in today's youth.'

He didn't look too controlled when he walked in at one thirty in the morning. He was singing 'Slow Boat To China' and Aunt Fran didn't even notice me picking fur off the sandwiches. She insisted they were 'beautiful'. Still, at least she looked perkier.

Aideen is still in bed. I'm going over to see Damien. Maybe he can help me work out what to do about Patrice. And then, later, I'll have to try and sort out the microwave. Mum hasn't seen that yet. Some clown stuck an apple in it and turned it on full. It will take hours to shift all that burnt mess.

Forty-one

After yet another silent breakfast I decided I'd had enough of mum's endless sulking. The relatives have gone. Something odd happened. Aunt Fran knocked on my bedroom door just before she left and half came into the room.

'Yo,' I said all cheerily. She just stood there, and waited for me to come to her. I did. Then, pressing ten pounds in my hand, she said, 'I heard you're involved in a rehousing project.'

Obviously mum had been telling her about Trass, and the campaign we've started to try and get the council moving on the halting site and those infamous houses. Still nothing on that front.

'This might help a bit, buying stamps or something. I admire the way you young people get on and do things. Good Luck.'

She gave me a little hug, and went. Poor Aunt Fran.

Anyway, mum's pathetic sulking was getting me down. It's so childish. She's still harbouring a grudge about that sheepskin rug. Anyone would think I've become a radical activist and enlisted Patrice's help to mutilate the rotten table.

I walked early to school and the first person I encountered was Patrice, skulking around looking through unlocked lockers, reading people's copies they'd left behind by mistake. Why is she always at school so early?

'Patrice. I have a problem.' Scared as I was, I wanted the whole thing out in the open. Maybe it's because I don't want, ever, to be as apologetic as Aunt Fran. Something was driving me on.

She looked at me, slightly alarmed.

'It's you. You probably don't remember, but you scratched our table at home. The scratch is bad, but what you dug in, with whatever you chose to use, has deeply offended me. More than that, you've upset my mother.'

Students were beginning to arrive and Patrice's discomfort was growing. Usually she has one or two side-kicks with her but since Caroline's and Dora's defection she's resorted to a couple of first year girls, still spell-bound by her superiority. They weren't in school yet.

'What I need from you is an apology to my mother and a visit by you with some of that stuff you can buy in supermarkets - it's labelled mahogany - to help wipe out the mistake.'

Still saying nothing she looked round at everyone. I was beginning to feel unhappy about having her there, alone, on the spot. I'd been there too. This wasn't confrontation; it was now something different. My silent support group was there. They had quietly joined me, Damien, Enda, Catherine, Trass and Clara.

'You'll help us?' I asked them, praying that they hadn't had enough of trying to repair the damage of one very badly thought out party. A nod from Damien was all I needed.

'Ok. You buy the scratch gunge, bring yourself and an apology and we'll forget all about it.'

She came, two evenings later. She apologised. Mum was very gracious and disappeared out to the shop to buy treats. Patrice even made us laugh telling us stories about her father who's recently become a born again something or other religious group. It's not that being a born again anything is funny. He's welcome to do what he pleases, but burning the television and all Patrice's teenage magazines in the front garden can't have endeared him to the neighbours or his family.

Damien was right. Suspending her only made her life harder at home. Apparently her dad can get pretty angry. I read violent into that word. Patrice is thawing out, gradually.

Better still, despite our ignoble efforts (it was good fun though), mum has given away the table. It now resides in the coffee room at the University. She's bought a serviceable and very ancient monstrosity from the auction rooms.

'At least you can now stop complaining about my devastating your precious rain forests,' she explained, laughing.

She's right. The wood from the old trees that made the table probably housed monkeys and apes when the world was only just beginning to understand imbalance. I hope it's not all too late.

Forty-two

Ed has a new girlfriend. She's great. She's almost the opposite to Charlie. I hope Charlie is doing all right. I asked Ed if he still wrote to her but he said there wasn't much point. That's the problem, you get so close to someone and then when it's over, for whatever reason, it, the good times, are left behind. Ed needs someone else in his life. He's still a bit insecure, but he can be as insecure as he likes as long as people like Louise are around.

We were talking the other day and she wanted to know if it was difficult giving up meat.

'Not if you want to. I began for all the wrong reasons and then discovered a load of good reasons to carry it on.'

I explained about coming here, being very angry, using not eating meat, no, more than that, having to be treated differently, as a way of getting back at everyone.

'How do you say no at other people's houses? How do you not embarrass someone who has gone to a lot of trouble to make you a meal?'

'That's easy. Well, you can do it in one of two ways. Straight out, I'm a vegetarian. That can upset certain families. They assume you're a freak and proceed to treat you as one. Or there's the skating around the truth method. I know it's a lie but the first time I went back to Trass's I didn't know how to handle the situation. Sitting on the table was a chunk of bacon and cabbage and potatoes. Mrs Mac had heard they were to be considered for one of the houses. Trass was just about to say something when I explained that I was a hopeless eater who survived on potatoes. I didn't know then, I do now, that the whole lot was cooked in bacon water. I knew I wasn't going to starve. I'd spotted the apple tart as soon as I came in. Plus, baked beans and fruit and cheese, with brown bread would keep everything balanced nicely, once I got home. Mum continues to be obsessed with a balanced diet.

'After we'd cleared the table (the apple tart was like ambrosia), I told Mrs Mac the truth. She wasn't offended. She was interested. She asked me why I'd chosen Ireland, beef producing Ireland, to begin my quest into the joys of vegetarianism. I didn't choose Ireland. Oddly enough Ireland has chosen me.'

Louise laughed. She's easy to talk to. She's never been outside Cork. Everyone she knows, her family, her friends, they are all from round here. That's good for Ed.

Soon it will be Christmas, my first Christmas here and my second without dad. He's never far away from my thoughts but it's not like a pain now, it's an ache. You know when you have a toothache and you bite on a clove, the pain goes away for a while. Sometimes, when I'm sitting in Damien's room, or the gang are around here, or we're all walking somewhere, then I'm absorbed, temporarily anaesthetised. They are like the clove, working against the ache.

Mum has assured me that is how Peter and all her new friends are to her. For now, she says, she's working through being on her own but that she never stops remembering. She has her wedding and engagement ring in a little box, which every so often she opens and then closes, because she has to carry on. I do believe my mother is improving.

I had a chat with Mrs Morrow, the counsellor. She's sympathetic, but when she suggested that it was time to give back my pebble and the bit of wood from our old front door, I refused.

'Give it time,' she said.

Next year I'll be fourteen. That has to carry more weight than thirteen. I want to organize a group to change the school uniform. It's criminal to have to wear something as uncomfortable as that. I want to put pressure on the Councillors who make promises. Trass and her mum are still in the caravan. Everything takes too long. The people who count, the officials, are sitting in comfy houses, all organised. I intend to ruffle their feathers, with the help of Mrs K, mum and Mrs Mac. Those three are quite a trio.

I gave in. I cut my hair. I couldn't stand it any longer. You would think the hairdresser used a ruler, she's made the sides so straight. The relief of not having spikey bits stuck into my face is *huge*. I had to do a job on Puss's. I wanted to make him feel good. I don't think I'm cut out to be a hairdresser. Chopping away at all the bits of still glued-on flour has made him look a bit lop-sided. But his whiskers continue to bristle like antennae.

One day I'm super happy, the next I feel down. But the spots are going, gradually. I think I must have drunk a reservoir dry with all the water I've taken to drinking. It works.

I am Vanessa Carter, living in Ireland, born in England and I am a vegetarian. I think, with the help of my friends and my family, particularly my brother Ed and my mother, I will be just fine.

We'll be seeing Posie and Dorinda at Easter. I wonder what they are doing now? I hope, I really hope that they have changed. Because I know that I have!

BRIGHT SPARKS

HAS ANYONE SEEN HEATHER

Mary Rose Callaghan

Fast-moving THRILLER about two Irish teenage sisters' search for their mother, **Heather Kelly**, last heard of somewhere in London.

An absolutely believable story which tugs at the heart strings as **Clare** and **Katie** discover that life in London is no bed of roses.

"A thoroughly up-to-date teenage book... a breakthrough in Irish literature."
Margrit Cruickshank *The Irish Times*

£3.99

BRIGHT SPARKS

Winner of Reading Association of Ireland Special Merit Award

DAISY CHAIN WAR

Joan O'Neill

Set during the late thirties and early forties, this is the heartwarming story of cousins, Irish **Lizzie** and English **Vicky**, growing up during 'The Emergency'.

"**An** eye-opener for the young reader and a nostalgic treat for the older one." Robert Dunbar *The Irish Times*

"**An** exciting story about growing up during 'The Emergency' in Dublin. Definitely a good read for girls of twelve and over." Blathnaid Archer *Sunday Press*

£4.99

Attic Press hopes you enjoyed **I'm a Vegetarian**.
To help us improve the **BRIGHT SPARKS** series
for you please answer the following questions.

1. Did you enjoy this book? Why?

_____

_____

_____

2. Where did you buy it?

_____

_____

3.What did you think about the cover?

_____

_____

4. Have you ever read any other books in the BRIGHT
SPARKS series? Which one/s?

_____

_____

_____

If there is not enough space for your answers on this coupon continue on
a sheet of paper and attach it to the coupon.

Post this coupon to **Attic Press**, 4 Upper Mount Street, Dublin 2 and we'll
send you a **BRIGHT SPARKS** bookmark and a free copy of our catalogue.